The Texas Ranger and the Professor

by

Susan Payne

The Texas Ranger and the Professor

The Wild Rose Press, Inc.
PO Box 708
Adams Basin, NY 14410-0708
Visit us at www.thewildrosepress.com

Publishing History
First Cactus Rose Edition, 2020
Trade Paperback ISBN 978-1-5092-3295-6
Digital ISBN 978-1-5092-3296-3

Published in the United States of America

Edwards closed his eyes again, desperately saying a prayer to help him not piss this woman off and have his commanding officer tear a strip off his hide when she went off irritated complaining to him. "Ma'am, I'm used to the desert terrain and all the unfriendly things that live there, whereas you…." He perused her from the tips of her stylish boots to the top of her head adorned with a small box trimmed with a little bird and branch of fake cherries, which passed as a hat. "Are simply not."

"You know nothing about me, sir. I am more than capable of traveling on my own as long as the supplies I requested have been furnished to me." She went to sidestep him in dismissal as she saw the mule piled with items she seemed to recognize.

"Ma'am, I can't allow you to do that. Ranger mules are not to be trusted with strangers and often seem docile when they are planning their worse revenge," he told her to warn her away from the ornery pack animal.

Dr. Reeves glanced into his face. "You are joking, right? Now you are trying to frighten me with a mule? I can handle anything with a bridle, believe me." She again went to step around his tall muscular frame.

Dedication

To my lovely daughters for the hours of reading and encouragement with which they always supported me.

Other Stories by Susan Payne

Harrison Ranch & Macgregor's Mail Order Bride
Sweetwater Series, Book One

A Midwife for Sweetwater & A New Face in Town
Sweetwater Series, Book Two

Jeremy's Home & There's Always Hope
Sweetwater Series, Book Three

New Banker in Town & Happy Endings
Sweetwater Series, Book Four

The Persistent Marquess

Forever Kind of Woman

Rescued by a Highlander

Southwest Texas 1879

CHAPTER ONE

"Capt'n Edwards, sir. Permission to enter," a young male called from outside the tent.

"Permission granted, Ranger, and I told you not to use my rank any longer," he said huskily. "I muster out in less than a month." He rubbed his hand over his face, trying to relieve the eyestrain from staring at small print for so long, stroking his mustache and day's growth of stubble lining his jaw. Getting ready to take the bar exam was grueling work. He combed his fingers through his hair trying to make himself more presentable. He didn't make much of an example for a young recruit.

A slender man, dressed as well as any city dandy minus his cravat stepped into the exceptionally neat tent. "Ah, Ranger Edwards, sir, I was hoping to be able to attend the Major's dance this evening and I have come up short in my required dress. Bailey was the last one of us to get to go out. He got gravy on the tie and didn't clean it so now there isn't one available in time for the festivity."

Edwards huffed out a breath as he stood, his head brushing the top of his tent and took the two steps to the wooden trunk at the foot of his cot. Bending, he opened it, lifting the neatly ironed shirts and setting them on the pile of vests next to them. Taking out a clean, pressed black tie he handed it to the young Ranger.

"You know how to tie it, Meijers?"

1

"Yes, sir. I just don't have one. Got left somewhere when we departed San Antonio, I guess. Anyways, we have enough clothes for three of us to go to the dance and not embarrass the Rangers. I'm putting my next pay into civilian clothes. I'm tired of having to keep wearing trousers and coats that don't quite fit right. Then I can wash my other ones all at once and have a clean outfit set aside."

"A commendable endeavor, lad," Edwards said, although he wasn't much older than the man in front of him. He had been younger than Meijers when he started with the Rangers over six years earlier. It was times like this that made him know leaving the service to the newer recruits was the right choice.

"Thank you for the use of the tie, sir. I'll make sure it's cleaned and pressed before I get it back to you."

"No hurry. I've been given a special assignment. I've got to babysit some guy who wants to go out into the desert around here and paint pictures of the flora and fauna. Pulled some strings with his uncle or something who's a federal Senator." He rubbed his already messed hair once again. "God save me from the city do-gooders who think just because they paint some pretty pictures of a coyote the ranchers aren't still gonna want to shoot the dumb things' head off when it chases their calves."

"He coming into town on the train then, sir?" asked Meijers as he tied a passable bow after wrapping the material around his neck twice.

"Hell, no. Say's the train is one of the instruments of civilization that is cutting into the wild animal's habitat and living arena. That the noise, need for fuel and water caused by the steam engine eats away at the environment of the western frontiers' natural animals

2

and upsets the plant balance. Sounds like all malarkey to me. He's coming in by stage, but sent his stuff and a list of staples he wants packed onto a mule for the trip," Edwards said, sitting back in front of his desk to try to finish the treatise he had been reading when he was interrupted.

The younger man's interest was caught. "Like what kinds of staples and stuff?"

"I didn't bother reading the list. Sounded like a lot of crazy things, so I handed it off to the quartermaster. Told him he was in charge of getting everything on the list and packing it up for the trip tomorrow. I can't be chasing down every paint brush or special pot some citified know-it-all wants to take to keep the desert from seeming like the desert." Then said, more to get the young man to leave so he could get back to his reading, "You better get going or all the food will be gone by the time you get there."

Practically jumping to attention, the young Ranger said, "You're right, sir. Have a good night." The recruit left through the flap, letting it drop into place to keep what little heat the kerosene burner was giving off inside his canvas home.

The following day, he was waiting at the stagecoach office just as the stage pulled in, ready to offer the good doctor botanist or whatever he was, his last chance of having a beer. Edwards had been told not to expect to come back into town for two or three weeks depending on the number of plants and animals the man found to study.

Edwards perused the passengers as they disembarked, most eager to leave the odorous confines of the conveyance on this already hot Texas day. The first person off the stage was a very pretty blond with large blue eyes who Edwards would have chatted up if it were any other time. Then a more somber lady descended with brown hair pulled into a tight bun and large brown eyes whose gaze darted along the boardwalk, not landing on any one thing. A heavier man got out puffing, hopefully not the botanist since he was so out of shape, he would never make two weeks in the desert. He was followed by a slimmer, tall man with glasses and an expression on his face as if he smelled something rotting all the time. The last man, also thin, had grey hair mixed into his mutton chop whiskers and wore a diamond and gold ring. Edwards thought this wasn't a very good way to begin their trip, his not even being able to locate the man.

Stepping forward he asked the tall, lean man, "Dr. Jessie Reeves, I presume?" Putting his right hand out towards the thin man.

"*Nein, nein*, um not dat mon. Heinz, Erich Heinz," the tall man said, holding his own hands close to his chest as if Edwards were trying to take him into custody.

"Sorry," Edwards replied in the German he learned from another ranger so he could work with the large number of German immigrants in Texas, "My mistake entirely. I was looking for someone else."

Heinz relaxed immediate and returned in German, "That is all right, sorry to be so nervous. I heard bad things about Texas and thieves. But now I see the badge."

As Edwards was deciding which of the other men he was there to meet, both of whom were leaving the street after retrieving their bags, a pleasant female voice behind him said, "I'm Dr. Jessie Reeves and I presume you are Ranger Edwards?"

Edwards closed his eyes and turned slowly afraid of whom he would see when he opened them. If it was the pretty blond there was no way in hell, he'd trust himself alone with her out in the desert for weeks on end. He opened his eyes to find the serious appearing brunette with her right hand out to shake his larger one.

Edwards' hand swallowed hers up, but she was surprisingly strong and gave his hand an acceptably firm shake. Peering into her upturned face, he realized her eyes weren't brown but hazel, the green much more predominant as she gazed into the sunlight. "Sorry, ma'am. I wasn't told to be expecting a woman. I read your letter to my commanding officer and we assumed you were male. I'm afraid the arrangements that were made are not suitable for you, but I can arrange a room at a nearby hotel."

The petite woman wore a fancy striped beige and brown dress which allowed the bustle freedom to sway, making her waist seem so narrow his hands could span it. Smiling, but with a hint of steel, she said, "I could make arrangements at a hotel for myself, Ranger Edwards, as I've been doing since I turned sixteen if that is what I wanted or required. I sent a very specific list requesting what I would need. If you do not wish to accompany me that is acceptable to me. The escort of a Ranger was at my uncle's request not mine. So, if you will point me towards my mount and supplies, I'll be off."

Edwards closed his eyes again, desperately saying a prayer to help him not piss this woman off and have his commanding officer tear a strip off his hide when she went off irritated complaining to him. "Ma'am, I'm used to the desert terrain and all the unfriendly things that live there, whereas you…." He perused her from the tips of her stylish boots to the top of her head adorned with a small box trimmed with a little bird and branch of fake cherries, which passed as a hat. "Are simply not."

"You know nothing about me, sir. I am more than capable of traveling on my own as long as the supplies I requested have been furnished to me." She went to sidestep him in dismissal as she saw the mule piled with items she seemed to recognize.

"Ma'am, I can't allow you to do that. Ranger mules are not to be trusted with strangers and often seem docile when they are planning their worse revenge," he told her to warn her away from the ornery pack animal.

Dr. Reeves glanced into his face. "You are joking, right? Now you are trying to frighten me with a mule? I can handle anything with a bridle, believe me." She again went to step around his tall muscular frame.

At this point Edwards realized several interested people had stopped to watch and listen to the drama beginning to unfold in the street. "Sorry, Ma'am, where were my manners. Please come into the shade of the boardwalk and I'll see about finding you a refreshing cool drink." He tried to lead her out of the public's view.

"I'm going into the hotel where I will purchase a bath and then I will be ready to travel to our first stop for the night." She turned to the coachman, pointed and said, "That bag's mine. Here's something for your trouble." She grabbed the bag and headed towards the hotel before Edwards could find any way of countering her plan.

Edwards saw Dr. Reeves leave the hotel's front

doors while she ignored him as he sat rocking back in a chair on the boardwalk. He was watching the activities in the street and trying to figure out what he could say to keep this single minded, un-natural woman in town where she would be safe, where both of them would be safe. He stopped with his first argument that she would not have access to the amenities she was used to while in the desert. He looked her up and down. The frilly city girl was gone and a sensible Texan woman was in her place.

Dr. Reeves now wore a long-sleeved shirt with vest much as Edwards had on. Her leather skirt was split so she could ride a western saddle and the knee-high boots that showed beneath it were suitable for riding and desert walking. There was a bandana around her neck to pull up in case of a sand storm and a wide brimmed ten-gallon Stetson with string tie hanging down under her chin.

She had already pulled on her leather riding gloves. "Is everything ready then, Ranger?"

"Yes, Dr. Reeves, right this way. I had a stopping place already in mind and we can still make that if we don't need to rest too often," he said, surrendering to the enemy for the first time in his Ranger's career, in fact, in his life.

She stood in front of the mule her brows drawn down in concern. "This mule is a little small. Are you sure the pack isn't too heavy for him?"

"No, he's fine. He seems small, but he can haul a lot of weight. Don't worry about him." He said, defending the smaller mules the Ranger divisions favored.

Edwards went to help the doctor into her saddle, but she was seated by the time he got there. Instead, shrugged and mounted his own horse, taking the leading rein to the mule with him. He turned his horse and the pack mule followed as did the doctor, having no trouble guiding her mount and kicking it into the faster trot Edwards was setting for them as they left the town behind.

There wasn't much talking. Edwards in the lead, letting himself turn enough to catch the doctor's profile. He could see if she was doing all right and not showing any signs of fatigue. They did stop to rest the horses and mule and to let them drink from one of the few sources of water they would find on this trip although he planned for their longer stop to be near a stream. At least it was there this time of year. He had known it to be dry some seasons if it had been hot.

Jessie gazed around, observing the relative lushness of the landscape near the water as opposed to the less dense and friendly foliage of plants further into the desert. As the sun began to set, she realized they must have been approaching the area the Ranger had mentioned and was glad she could get off the horse and remain off for the next few hours.

She needed to prove to others, especially her colleagues that a woman could do field work as well as a male. If she failed in any aspect of this project, she would never be able to apply for any other. She had fought for this assignment even though it was beneath her qualifications as a professor simply to prove a woman could go into harsh terrains and complete a study without running home scared. The fact that this desert was one of the safest places she had studied was lost on the men who handed out the awards and grants. It wasn't a test of her ability and training, but it was a test she knew she had to surpass.

She felt apprehensive about the coming night. Always taking the weight of a pack into consideration when setting up the provisions for a trip, her plans included a two-man tent. She had always shared those accommodations with her guide although her guides were usually wizened old men hired for their knowledge of a territory rather than brawn.

Her escort on this trip definitely did not fall into that category. She couldn't find anything about him comparable to those others and she couldn't change what was already done. She mentally chastised herself for not considering this outcome, but her uncle had surprised her with the information she would have a Ranger escort at the last minute. For some reason, her guardian decided she needed one on this comparatively short study. Of course, most of the other trips had been in conjunction with her father, even if they were to more dangerous and remote areas than the Texas desert.

Watching surreptitiously, Edwards, wearing a cavalry style shirt and wool trousers, strode toward the mule. He wore his side arm on a separate belt lined with bullets and his leather vest boasted a Ranger badge on the right side. High leather boots with spurs, the extra-large rowels jingling with each step, made up the rest of his desert outfit. She couldn't deny his virility or her acknowledgement of it.

He was handsome, no getting around that. His hair was a little long for her taste, but his mustache was trimmed and free of food. He kept his nails clean. Two things she felt necessary to maintain a civilized presence. His eyes were his best feature and he used his brows to convey most of his emotions even if he wasn't aware of it. She didn't have to hear his words when she annoyed him. The height of his brows from his eyes indicated everything she needed to know.

Jessie came to a decision. She would treat the attractive Ranger as she would any other guide. He was there to assist her to find the area, setup camp and keep watch for poisonous snakes and arachnids. Jessie would be able to conduct her study and be the professional she was. For years she had been fighting the stigma of being a woman in what is considered a man's field. This trip would go a long way in proving she could work alongside men and not have it compromise her research.

As soon as she dismounted, Edwards came and took the reins from her. "I'll take them and hobble them a little way away. I'll get the fire started as soon as I get back. We'll need to eat and set up camp before it gets cold which comes on quickly here in the desert."

By the time he got back, Jessie had started the fire as well as having a small pile of starter branches. She was getting up to find some larger pieces that would keep the fire hot enough for cooking.

"I don't suppose you could get the coffee started while I gather some larger limbs?" the Ranger asked, evidently planning to do a lot of the work to keep them from starving or freezing.

"I can do that. Just let me see how the pack is set up. I found the food but not the cooking gear." She bent over the pile of items the Ranger had taken off the mule and rummaged through the many sacks and boxes.

The aromatic smell of beef stew greeted Edwards as he returned to camp. His mouth watered because if it tasted anywhere as good as it smelled, he was going to enjoy this meal a whole lot more than he usually did meals cooked out in the open when he was on an assignment.

"You order that?" He nodded toward the pot bubbling over the reddish gold coals.

"No, merely all the ingredients. A few spices and dried herbs add a whole new aspect to a can of cooked beef." She checked the biscuits to make sure they weren't burning on the bottom then moved the covered pan back into the coals, this time upside down.

"It's about ready, Ranger, if you are."

"I'm starving now that I've got a whiff of this meal." He sat down waiting for her to finish filling the pie plate in front of her.

Jessie passed it on to him, setting two of the browned biscuits leaning against the rim. "I ordered enough food then doubled it. I found that when I was out on safari or climbing the Grand Tetons or hiking in the Himalayas, I always had a ferocious appetite."

Edwards didn't stand on ceremony and started spooning the aromatic and delicious stew into his mouth but stopped to ask, "You telling me you visited all those places? Bragging?"

"A little," she answered honestly. "And I want you to know I am not a delicate female. I won't wilt, run or faint at the sight of blood. I've been to Africa, China and other fantastic places anyone could dream of travelling. I wasn't simply visiting them I was studying them. Exotic people and places are my passion. It's not always easy to get there or to stay there, but I always have."

She turned her attention to her plate and offered him the rest of what was in the pot. When the meal was over, she placed a cup of hot coffee in his hands. He thought he could get used to this. As the warmth left the earth and the cold changed places with it, he searched the campsite for a place to sleep.

"I'll get the pot and dishes cleaned out with sand if you can get started on the tent. I'll help if you need me to, but I figure a Ranger can set up a simple tent." She surprised him by giving him the lead in setting up the camp.

The tent was already separated from the rest of the packed items. He opened it on the one spot he thought had any protection from the winds that could blow across the desert floor this time of year. He had it staked out by the time Jessie was done and the food packed away to discourage nosy varmints from visiting.

She carried the shovel with her past the light thrown from the fire's coals. "I'll be over to the left, but I've got my hand gun with me if I run across something mean."

Edwards stayed where he was, deciding he would have the one cigarette he allowed himself a day. He lit it against one of the grey ash coals and blew out a plume of smoke. He almost crushed it out when Jessie appeared from the darkness, but she stopped him.

"Don't put it out on my account. My father smoked a pipe and I always enjoyed the aroma of tobacco around a campfire. Made me think of home and now it makes me think of him."

"So, it was your father who urged you in your conquests of the continents?" He took another draw on his cigarette.

"Both my parents. I was born crossing the Atlantic. They thought they could make it home to Philadelphia in time, but then there I was, a surprise in more ways than one. My parents had only been married six months and I was not a six-month baby," she announced proudly.

Edwards smiled in the darkness. She probably was proud of it. Proud of all the non-traditional events of her life and he didn't fool himself into thinking there weren't more than a few. "So, Philadelphia is home?"

"No, I told you I was born in the middle of the Atlantic. Philadelphia was my parents' home, at least for a while. I learned to walk in Constantinople, I learned my catechism in Rome, and I learned to love anthropology everywhere I went."

"So, you're not a botanist? You consider yourself an anthropologist?" He wanted to get it right, but he wasn't sure why. After all, what did it really matter to him? In a couple of weeks, she'd be back east and he'd be out of the Rangers.

"I am an anthropologist who feels everything in an animal's habitat, which includes homo sapiens, influences that animals' lifecycle. The way it's born, the way it matures, the way it mates and the way it dies. Everything is part of everything else, all animals are intertwined and affecting other animals where one touches another, like a snake pit swarming with vipers."

Warming to her subject she continued, "No viper bites another, for if they did it would send off a chain reaction and all the vipers would be dead as a result. I'm out to study living things so we won't be tempted to bite before we know what that bite will mean to the rest of the animals around us, including mankind."

"Interesting, gives me something to think about tonight. Thanks, Doc. Have a good night." He leaned back against his saddle to soak in what heat the coals were able to throw his way.

13

"You don't plan on sleeping out in the open, Ranger?"

"I not only planned on it. I'm doing it." He chuckled.

"Then I will be cold, too. This tent is sized for two adults. The heat from both our bodies is needed to keep it warm enough to be comfortable in the cold desert nights. Are you saying you don't think two reasonable adults can share a tent to keep warm?" she asked, in that reasonable tone he was beginning to dread.

"No, Doc, I didn't think that far ahead. I only thought a reasonable woman wouldn't want a complete stranger to sleep next to her in a limited space." He wasn't sure where this argument left him. He could appear as if he didn't trust himself next to an attractive woman or he could be nonchalant and act like sharing a tent wasn't a big whoop, which, of course, it wasn't.

He could control himself around women, this woman. His commanding officer had given him a job to do and Edwards had never failed in completing an assignment in his career. After the moment's hesitation, he got up and kneeled to enter the tent's flap he had watched her fanny disappear through.

Her last jab before rolling up in her blanket leaving the other one for him was to say, "Remind me to tell you about the Chinese baths where a whole town, grandparents to babies would sit in huge tubs heated with fires burning under them, all naked as jay birds."

Edwards rolled over with his back to her and thought what a thing for her to say just before going to bed. Now how was he going to get the picture out of his mind of a bunch of old naked people bathing together? He wondered if that was her plan to keep his mind off being in a small tent next to someone of the opposite sex.

14

CHAPTER TWO

Watching as the doctor left the warmth of the two-person tent first, he heard her walk a few yards away. Edwards remained in the tent to get his morning arousal under control before presenting himself outside in the daylight. His early morning dreams had Dr. Reeves sitting in a bath waiting for him to join her so they could wash each other and then continue on to doing things that naked men and women have been doing to each other since the beginning of time. He fought down his wayward thoughts and was finally presentable by the time he heard her return to camp carrying a few dried branches to add to the still hot ashes.

"I'll get the smoked side-pork sliced and cooking if you will take care of the animals," Jessie said, seeing him out of the tent and ready for the day. "Afterwards, I plan on taking my sketch pad and measuring off a grid and drawing the plants within that grid. I'll do it over again until I have all the species documented. That way, when I or someone else returns in first five and then ten years, there will be a comparison grid for them to use. To chart whether plants have changed, increased or disappeared completely." She got out the fry pan and placed the sliced meat and raw onion into it.

It didn't take too long to feed the animals and toss their manure further from the campsite. "All this work you're planning on doing isn't for use right now? Won't be used for years?" he asked making sure he understood her work.

"These original inventories become very important as years go by. If we keep killing off certain animals and plants, they will be extinct by the first of the century. If not by then, at least, within the next hundred years. We won't get these animals and plants back. They will be as gone as the Dodo bird."

"So there really was a Dodo bird? I thought they were just folklore."

"No, like the Stellers Sea Cow, animals disappear. It has been hunted out of existence for its meat and leather, the last one sighted in 1786. Birds seem to be the most precarious with species being lost within my lifetime. Sometimes because their food source is gone, plowed under for civilization, or because of a new predator introduced to their environment."

Jessie broke the biscuits in half, laying them down in the hot grease before placing the crisp meat with cooked onions on top. She handed him a pie plate with the drippings poured over the biscuits. Grabbing a spoon, he cut off a piece of the hot meat with biscuit and chewed slowly, enjoying the simple yet satisfying meal.

Jessie continued speaking, "The fact is these animals, like those sea cows, are so important that if one species dies off, it could mean a whole village dies. Some of the aboriginal people I have lived with were dependent on a single food or animal. Like our Prairie Indians and the bison. They had every aspect of their life linked to that one animal. When it was hunted to extinction, then the Indians had nothing to use in its place. Even the cattle that have been given to them can't mitigate the loss. So, the buffalo and the Plains Indians were decimated with the same long gun and bullet." Jessie continued eating.

"Now we're getting to a part I have some opinion about. I fought the Indians when they were killing the folks trying to settle Texas. They were brutal and incomprehensible in the torture that was propagated against the White and Spanish settlers. Taking slaves has been a way of life for them, stealing women and children to then misuse them and treat them worse than animals." He felt compelled to tell her his thinking but was unsure why. "I understand they were here first, but I also know the Comanche killed off the original tribes who were here before they came. The Apache were driven into Mexico and they are still sending raiding parties into Texas. The Rangers are often ordered to take back an area from the tribes and help the settlers get a safe place to live."

"I agree there seems to be some sort of natural order of things, a pattern of loss and renewal, replacement of one animal with another. I was in Indiana and studied a prehistoric animal skeleton. It was found in a river bed as the moving water eventually uncovered it and then archeologists dug it up." She began to clean out her dish with the desert sand. "Its size alone makes me think it may have eaten itself out of hearth and home. The animal ate all the food it was used to and was left with starvation because it couldn't find anything to replace that one kind of plant." She gathered her implements needed to line off a grid for study.

"Is there anything I can do to help?" He began to feel redundant.

"No, I'm pretty self-sufficient with all of this since I have done it so often, first helping my father and now on my own." Seeming to be ready to work she added, "I hope you brought something to keep yourself busy."

"I did bring my books in case we got early evenings. I can work on those or work on my maps."

"Maps?"

"I'm a cartographer, an explorer, if you will. Some of the maps the government uses aren't always accurate. Building the railroads proved that. New maps and topographies are required so we can have more current information." He took a leather rolled scroll carrier from his saddlebag.

She walked towards the area she was going to study first and began to pound in a short stake. "I don't break for a midday meal, but feel free to eat what you want. I put out beans to soak and set aside some of the cooked side pork and onions to add to them later."

"I can do that. Beans are one of the things I can cook well." He was smiling as he sat down to unroll his maps.

Edwards watched Jessie as she began her work and marveled at her ceaseless energy and fortitude to do work that was usually set aside for males. She bent and measured and laid string and did it again till she had four sides. Then she pulled out the sketch pad and sat down, studying one of the plants as if she had never seen the small succulent before in her life. She spent quite a lot of time drawing that plant, as Edwards kept glancing up from his work to make sure she wasn't in need of his aid.

Finally, as the sun started to disappear into the western sky, Jessie came back to the campsite. "Were you able to accomplish anything today?"

"I feel I got something of worth done. And you, did you make a good start?"

"I have three plants drawn and measured. I'll give

each a code number and when I find that plant again, I won't need to draw it, only measure it and add the code. That way, as I finish more drawings the next grids will take less time, simply needing the codes and sizes put in their spot." Washing her hands, she sat down and ate the meal Edwards had finished preparing.

The next few days passed much the same way. Edwards was at first surprised, as the two became in tune with one another's methods and working together, as if long used to each other. The evenings were spent with one trying to convert the other to their way of thinking. Jessie showing the danger signs of man's interfering with the normal balance in the animal and plant world. He was eager to bring her thinking around to his, that opening up new territory to settlers was how the world and man would grow and was the natural progression of mankind.

Nights were spent in the shared tent and it was working out better than Edwards thought at first. He enjoyed listening to Jessie's soft little snores when she slept on her back and had found he could control his more obstinate body parts although he found his hand on her hip more than once as he curled around her in his sleep. Jessie never mentioned it even if she knew it had happened. He liked that about her. She was down-to-earth and practical. There was no way around it. He couldn't believe she hadn't been born a Texan.

Jessie had exchanged her leather riding skirt for men's trousers, but Edwards grew used to seeing her derriere outlined as she crawled into the tent each night. He began to think women should be allowed to wear trousers if they wanted, made more sense than those silly corsets and bustles.

"I think I've done about all I can here. I haven't found a new plant species the entire last grid I did. It was simply codes and I have enough areas represented for a study. We should probably move the campsite in the morning."

"You're the boss, Doc. I'm just here to make sure you don't get lost and ensure you get back safe."

The second camp was near a stream that was large for the area they were studying. Edwards tried his hand at catching fish and finally got a couple of trout although they were not in their prime since they had come upstream to spawn. Jessie checked out the plants in the riverbed and along the banks, finding new species she dedicatedly drew and studied for posterity.

After dinner was their time to socialize, both of them busy with their drawings or studies during the daylight hours. Edwards would often smoke his one cigarette of the day and Jessie would inundate him with questions about Texas and its history, which Edwards knew a lot about. This evening, though, Edwards was turning the tables and questioning Jessie's knowledge or rather her opinion on human sociality.

"So, you're sitting there telling me it's actually the female of any species that makes the selection of a mate while the male just takes what he can get? That doesn't seem to me to be the way humans do things." He knew she would jump to argue against him. He enjoyed their verbal sparring, which might have been the attorney in him coming out.

"Most males are prettier than their female mates, especially birds. Some species actually bring gifts or make a nest that the female has the option of accepting or moving on to the next male's offerings. The female seeks specific attributes she wants in a mate."

"Even women, they have a specific type of man that meets their criteria?" He began to be intrigued with what Jessie would think was important in a mate. "Like what kind of things?"

"Well, anthropologically speaking, size is probably most important," she stated resolutely.

Edwards's eyebrows rose with surprise that Jessie would be so out spoken and listened intently.

"The strength and size of the male is important because it shows the female he will be a good provider and protector. Arm muscles would indicate his ability to throw a spear or wrestle an animal to the ground. Strong legs and buttocks indicate he can run an animal down or he will be virile, the thrusting muscles of importance for the reproductive act." Edwards would have sworn she had rosy cheeks, but her voice wasn't showing any signs of embarrassment.

"You're telling me women really consider those male body parts when seeking a mate?" He knew he sounded as doubtful as he felt.

"Not like checking off a list. The more civilized we become the more women realize an intelligent man is more important in our world, but I'm afraid we are as shallow as men when it comes to looking primarily at physical attributes." She continued to explain, "Take clothing, for instance. Men used to wear hose to emphasize the calf and thighs while skirts were popular in many cultures showing the entire bare male leg."

"What do men look for in women? I mean, beside facial beauty?"

"A pleasant face is an asset, but men take note of the size of the breasts to ensure the feeding of his offspring and the width of the hips to ensure they be of ample size for giving birth." This time there was no doubt her cheeks were as red as a ripe apple. "And that she is smaller than him. The human male likes to be larger and taller than his mate."

There was quiet for a moment as Edwards tried to decide whether or not she was teasing him, then thought she was probably telling him the truth. "I don't know if I looked at a woman as a baby-maker first and a partner second. I do know I better put an end to this kind of conversation before we head off to bed or I may embarrass myself." He made the statement in the casual way they had of speaking to one another after living in such close quarters for over two weeks.

"I'll get comfortable while you cool down. Remember you started this discussion." She crawled into the tent's flap, her fanny wiggling enticingly.

Edwards rolled and lit another cigarette thinking over the last conversation, clinically, not trying to stay aroused. He didn't want that kind of thinking intruding on his relationship with Doc. He liked being friends. He had never thought he could be friends with a woman, any woman and now he began to see the benefits. Men tried to persuade other men to their way of thinking, and if they couldn't they just tussled each other to the ground until one of them changed their mind. If a woman disagreed with a man, then the man had to find the facts and ideas that supported his belief. They may never see eye-to-eye, but Doc, at least, never made him feel as if he were wrong. Just that he hadn't persuaded her to his way of thinking. She wasn't being emotional, no blackmail of withholding herself from their camaraderie, no pouting. She stated her reasons and waited for him to come to the same conclusion due to his own intelligence.

Was he being manipulated? Probably, but he was also enjoying himself. Possibly, too much.

One night after a long day, the two of them were sitting around the fire and Jessie let her curiosity override her proper upbringing. "Your voice is relaxing to listen to, but it isn't natural is it? I mean, something changed your voice, probably after puberty."

"You asking or telling, Doc?"

"I'm asking, I guess. Rude of me, I know, but I never could stand an unanswered question." She was smiling at him in the low glow of the embers wanting to know more about him personally.

"I was out alone, searching for any signs of Indian unrest. Comanche to be exact. There had been sightings and cattle had been slaughtered. Many times, these small raiding parties attack the ranches themselves, stealing food, horses and taking captives. That's why the Rangers have to be so vigilant, because once a group starts up they can do a lot of damage in a short amount of time. Comanche don't just steal to feed themselves. They steal to drive the settlers out, make them retreat to the towns and forts."

He lit his one cigarette for the day and continued. "I saw the raiding party and I knew my only chance was to out run them. Trouble was they saw me at the same time. I was on a fast horse, but not faster than theirs with lighter riders and no saddle weight to hold them back. They caught up with me."

Jessie didn't want to make him remember bad times, but they hadn't gotten to the point of why his voice was so husky. "But you got away. You slipped past them or something?"

"Or something. They put a rope around my neck to walk me back to their camp, although they were going at a good pace, more than a man could keep up with. When I stumbled and fell, I was dragged behind the horse trying not to let my windpipe get crushed and hoping not to pick up too many cactus spikes along the way." He related the incident as if he were speaking of someone else.

"How horrible for you. Then they let you go?" she asked, deep down knowing it wouldn't have been that easy.

Edwards gazed at her. "Yeah, then they let me go."

She knew she would have nightmares for the rest of her life if he told her the truth and what did the truth matter now? She had her answer as to why his voice was all but gone – only a husky whisper, at most. "I'm sorry you went through any of it. And I'm stronger than I appear. I could have taken the whole truth, but perhaps it's just as well we let it lie. It isn't a good bedtime story, I'm sure." She removed her boots before crawling into the tent for the night.

After following their normal morning rituals, Edwards, now having a full beard and longer hair, headed to sit where he could watch Jessie work as she went to kneel down near the stream's banks. She focused on drawing the small water plants she found so fascinating. Knowing that during some months of the year this stream was much smaller or even dry, she was concentrating on the fragile vegetation.

Edwards felt their presence before he saw them, but it was too late. A Comanche tomahawk grazed his head as he tried to duck. He could see two other braves grab Jessie by the arms and restrain her from running to him. Then he felt two more hard blows land on his shoulder and back as he was beaten to the ground. This was the worst scenario he could have imagined when he first accompanied Jessie out into this wilderness.

He was half-conscious as two braves pushed him up onto his saddle-less horse, hands tied in front of him. He forced himself to peek through an eye swollen shut. He let out a relieved breath when he saw Jessie, her hands bound, sitting upright on her horse. The horse and loaded mule were being led by one of the painted braves as they set off from the camp towards the west, further away from civilization and the Ranger encampment. He tried to stay alert, not putting it past the Comanche to kill him out-right if he fell off the horse and then Jessie would have no one to help her through the agony to come.

A couple of hours passed or so Edwards thought since he wasn't completely aware of time as he passed in and out of consciousness. He knew they were close to the Comanche's camp. He could tell by the way the men were sitting straighter and the way they held their weapons with pride.

He maintained his seat on the horse as they headed toward the small group of tipis on the horizon. It appeared to be a small family clan broken off from the larger tribe on the reservation. That made them criminals and not afraid to break all the Whiteman's rules and treaty conditions. Probably young braves balking at the limited choices they now had to live with. Conditions they felt their weaker elders had agreed to. But each Comanche had a voice, a vote, and if a brave didn't agree, he was free to leave and start over with a new clan, a new tribe until the Rangers came down on them with a vengeance and wiped them off the face of the earth.

The small group of five braves, wearing breechcloths and moccasins, their tattooed bodies covered in many colors from the desert clays and their two captives stopped in the center of the camp as a few older braves, squaws and children came forward to observe what would happen to the two Whites.

The squaws of various ages, their hair pulled into odd tufts with painted faces, were wearing buckskin poncho styled blouses and fringed skirts with leggings. Some of them had their hair in two braids with colored cloth woven through them as they glared with contempt at Jessie's clothes. She was wearing the more sensible trousers with her hair blowing free, her hat left on the stream's bank along with her notebook and sketch pad.

One of the squaws grabbed Jessie's leg and pulled her off the horse to the ground, making her land hard on her knees as she was unable to get her feet under her in time to prevent the fall. The group of squaws laughed at what they saw as her poor horsemanship, given that they were expert riders since childhood. Jessie managed to get to her feet but wasn't allowed to move toward Edwards as he too, was shoved from his horse, landing on his back on the baked desert sand.

The braves argued amongst themselves and both Edwards and Jessie were shoved toward one of the tipis and pushed into the open flap that was pulled closed from outside.

CHAPTER THREE

The couple found themselves on a buffalo hide, a little smelly, but a softer landing than Edwards had feared. He tried to see in the dimness, searching for anything that could be used as a weapon but knew it would be fruitless. There was no way he could fight off the band of braves and take Jessie with him and he sure as hell wasn't leaving her behind. He would stay and take whatever he could to lessen her suffering.

"Oh, Edwards, your head is bleeding again, let me look at it." Jessie tried to see the gash at his temple.

"It'll stop in a minute, just got broke open. We have to talk. I need to explain things to you and we don't have a lot of time." He crawled close to her, whispering so the Comanche outside the tipi couldn't hear them.

"What are they going to do with us? I don't know much about this tribe, yet. Is there some way to barter with them? Buy our freedom?" Jessie faced the danger, the physical threat, with the bravery he came to expect from her.

He listened trying to make out some word or phrase from outside the tipi.

"They're fighting over you." At Jessie's quick gasp, he continued, "No, that's good. It really is. If the braves want you, they will argue about the fairest way to decide who gets you and they won't trade you across the border. The longer you stay with this band, the better chance you have of being found by the Rangers."

27

"The Rangers will come for us?"

"Of course, and they never give up. You'll be rescued and taken home so never give up," he told her honestly.

"You keep talking about me. What about you?"

"We both need to understand I'll probably be dead by tonight. There is no love lost between me and the Comanche. They will be after revenge for everything the Whiteman has ever done," he whispered hoarsely.

Edwards held her closer with his tied hands and whispered into her ear, "You're strong. I know you can endure this. Never give up hope of being rescued, the Rangers will hunt for you till they find you and take you home. Remember your uncle will offer a reward to get you back and the Comanche have few friends. Everyone they trade with or who rides near this camp are your possible rescuers. Make yourself apparent. Cut your hair short so you will stand out from the squaws. They may punish you, but they won't kill you. You're a valuable commodity."

In a rush, he continued to give her advice for her life among the Comanche. "Stay away from the squaws whenever possible. They are very jealous of White women and will cut or burn you, trying to get you to raise a hand to them so they can complain to the chiefs and have you beaten. Don't retaliate, no matter how provoked." He hesitated, knowing this was going to be difficult to say. "If you find yourself with child, no matter how many braves have taken you, claim the highest-ranking brave is the father. He will take you to his tipi and he will have the women in his family care for you. He'll protect you from the other braves and squaws. Take advantage of that if you're able."

Jessie didn't say anything, but he felt her trembling and hated he had to frighten her even more, but it had to be done so she would be prepared.

"How do you know all this? How do you know what their plans are?" she asked through chattering teeth.

"I just do." Then answered more truthfully, "I know of a survivor, a beautiful woman who lived a full and wonderful life after being rescued by the Rangers."

"What will happen to you? What have you heard?" He knew she worried over his fate. He wished he could save her from what she would have to witness.

"I'm expendable and a trophy. I need to be brought to my knees and they'll plan a fitting way of killing me. I'm the hated Ranger. Over the years we have become sworn enemies, of this tribe anyway. The young bucks always want to show off when they break away from the main group. I will be perfect for these braves to earn the respect of their elders," he explained, trying not to be graphic, knowing that what she will see during the next few months will be enough for her to contend with. Edwards hoped it would only be for a few months before she was found by the Rangers he knew would be sent after them.

"Edwards, I'm really afraid I won't be able to hold on. I'll die before anyone finds me once you're gone."

He shook her, trying to keep her from going into shock. "You're stronger than that, Jessie, I know you are. You can and will live through this, for me, so I know they didn't win, not everything."

Jessie buried her head into his chest saying, "It's bad enough I'm going to be raped, probably by every brave out there…. I need your help, I need you to do something for me, before, before they come for me." She was

29

rushing her words, pleading with her eyes. "I've never…I'm a virgin. I can't be strong and noble and wait to be saved after something like that. I'm sorry, I'm not that strong, I know it."

"Sure, you are. You're the bravest, strongest woman I know. You're a survivor, too." He wanted to assure her. Prove she could live through this.

"Make love to me, Benjamin, right now. Don't let them get everything from me, from us. Please don't think about it, just do it. For my sanity, for me, don't leave me like this," she pleaded when he seemed to hesitate.

A second passed, seemingly forever. Then he bent his head and kissed her. She responded as passionately as he had ever dreamed of her doing and found the kiss immensely pleasing. For long moments both participants seemed to have gotten lost in the kiss, his pelvic pushing her unto her back as he took control and brought a hand up to palm her breast, feeling a nipple harden and respond to the simple friction.

Edwards buried his hand in her hair, holding her as if he thought she would leave him, leave him before he could do what he had been dreaming of doing for days, weeks. He pushed aside her shirt's collar with his chin finding the waiting pebble with his mouth. Arching up to him, she begged without words that she wanted him to touch more of her body.

Understanding, he responded then felt her hands between them as she undid her belt and trousers, pushing them down, wiggling under him which enflamed his rigid manhood even more. She began to work on his belt when he leaned onto one hip and made short work of his clothes that seemed to be in the way.

"Are you certain this is what you want, Jessie?" he asked unsure now they were this close.

At her nod he placed his manhood between her legs, which were warm and waiting, finding her ready for him.

"Benjamin, I want it to be you. Don't leave me."

He pushed into her without further hesitation, knowing time was running out for them.

Covering the cry that escaped her mouth with his own, he continued to move as she caught the motion and moved with him until he felt her tighten involuntarily around him and he felt her spasms as he filled her with his seed.

He didn't let them lay there long after their climax, afraid the quiet outside the tipi meant the braves had made their decisions and were coming for them. He didn't want to have them take out any more anger on Jessie than they were already apt to do. Once they were both re-dressed, he held her close, but all the talking had been done. Now, he had to find any way to help her through this before they killed him.

"Thank you, thank you, Benjamin. I'll never be able to thank you enough for that." She buried her head into his shoulder.

"You gave me a precious gift. As a man with only a couple more hours to live, I'm very grateful. If it helps you make it through this ordeal then I will die knowing I made your captivity easier."

"You have, believe me, you have. I will hold on to these last few minutes until I am free again. Don't leave me, not until you have to." He moved away as she finished.

"They're coming for us. It's time to be courageous. Don't respond to anything they do to me. It only encourages them to take more drastic actions." He stopped talking after rolling away from her to be grabbed and hauled to his feet by three braves, all appearing to want both of the Whites dead or worse.

Once outside, both Edwards and Jessie closed their eyes to shield them from the bright sunlight. Jessie was forced to stand to the side of the tipi while the five braves formed a half circle with their focus on Edwards, his hands still bound loosely in front of him.

"Your mothers are dog faces," he called out to the braves in their own language.

Four braves looked toward the one in the center and waited for his response. He laughed asking how the white devil knew their language so well. The others seemed interested in the answer, as well, as they too laughed.

Edwards ignored the question. "And your fathers pee squatting like the squaws they are." He jeered at them openly.

That got their attention and the middle brave hit Edwards with the side of his spear pole, making Edwards bend with the pain and weight of the blow. The others whooped their encouragement for their member's show of strength. The brave jumped up and down in his enjoyment of inflicting pain to his enemy, even if he were merely playing with Edwards at this point. It was going to get more interesting for the braves in a little while.

The braves spoke to each other, sending taunting words and looks towards Edwards and Jessie. Edwards turned toward Jessie. "The winner of this battle, the brave that kills me will win you as the prize. I'll make sure the chief, the one with the breast plate, is the one who makes the fatal blow. You'll be safest with him."

"Don't Edwards, stay with me," she pleaded unable to keep her promise of not showing emotion or pain.

The brave closest to Edwards sliced through the leather thongs tying his hands together with one swing and then tore off Edwards' vest and shirt. Another brave cut the long underwear from the captive's upper torso, leaving streaks of blood where the skin was sliced as well. Once stripped to their satisfaction, they shoved Edwards into the center of the small circle formed by the braves while the rest of the villagers watched from the outside.

Jessie stared at the ground, trying not to let her gaze follow the long legs up his body when she found Edwards standing in the center. She was wary of any movement from any of the braves, all of whom held weapons in both hands. Spears, tomahawks and wicked looking wooden tools with a large bulbous end, some having nails embedded into them with the sharp points facing out and each of the braves taunting and making feinted moves toward Edwards.

Then the chief decided to get serious. She could see the members of the tribe wanted a show of power and strength, they hungered for blood. He swooped past Edwards, slicing a gash that bled profusely as another brave ran past in the opposite direction, hitting the captive's injured shoulder once more. The third and fourth braves came at him in the center of the circle, one from each side and swung at Edwards as he shifted to miss the brunt of their strikes, taking one to the back of his calf and the other to his shoulder again.

Then things seemed to speed up after each brave had had their first swing at him. They came at him from all directions with various weapons. She could see Edwards forcing himself to stand and take more until he felt their blood lust was satisfied. Then he would let the chief finish him off to become the owner and protector of Jessie. She knew Edwards wasn't making it look too easy of a win, he had to fight to the end. He held up his arm or hands to break the blows that came at him. She cringed hearing the bones in his hand snap, seeing the blood trickle down his back as the jabs from the spears and knifes did their damage.

Finally, Edwards was swaying on his feet, staring daggers at the braves as he taunted the chief about his masculinity and inability to do anything to hurt a Ranger. Enraged, the chief raised his tomahawk the blade held high and the target Edwards's head as that man dropped his protective arms and awaited the fatal blow.

A rifle shot rang out and the chief fell forward, just missing Edwards with the tomahawk's blade.

Then all hell broke loose as squaws and children ran crying and screaming into the tipis and the surrounding desert. Rangers rode in, hand guns firing, dropping every Comanche warrior they could find as they rounded up the women running and trying to escape from their worst enemy, the dreaded Texas Rangers.

Standing from where she had collapsed upon thinking Edwards was dead, Jessie ran to him then tried to stop the flow of blood from the worse of his wounds. He was unconscious, unaware the Rangers had rescued both of them. Heedless that his noble sacrifice had been interrupted, that he didn't need to endure any more pain or give up his life merely to lessen her anguish or injuries.

"Benjamin, Benjamin, please stay with me. Don't die. We are both going to be all right, don't leave me." But the man who stood so stoically for so long didn't have the strength to open his eyes to acknowledge if he heard her.

A young Ranger came and kneeled down beside her and Edwards. "Is the Captain dead? Did we get here too late?"

He cut her bindings as she spoke. "He's still breathing, but I don't know for how much longer. He has multiple injuries and some broken bones as well, probably cracked ribs. Can you take us back to our campsite if I tell you the way?" She tried to find enough material in Edwards' discarded shirt to cover the bleeding wounds.

"We came past your tent a couple of hours ago. We've been following this band of Comanche for the past two days. They got careless after capturing you and left a clean trail right to this camp although Captain Edwards might have had something to do with that. A lot of plants were bent over. Usually the Comanche are careful to have their horses do less damage."

"They were very excited to have captured us. I think they wanted to kill Ranger Edwards right from the start, but waited till we got here so they could show off for the others. Just the five who were in that raiding party got a chance to do this to him." Finally satisfied the emergency medical care was in place, she wanted to get Edwards back to where she had her medical bag. It hadn't been of interest to the Comanche when they went through the supplies.

"I need to check with my Captain, Ma'am, and then we can be on our way back. It's a long trip to town. If Captain Edwards is as bad off as he appears, a shorter trip is probably best." The young man named Meijers went to let his commanding officer know the plan.

The rest of the division took the shackled braves and squaws along with the young children on the long march to the fort. A trial would ensue and the braves who were there would be hung. The squaws and children would be returned to the reservation again. The tipis and their contents were set on fire, discouraging any other Comanche from using the same site. The war between the two people would continue.

They decided to use the Comanche's own method of carrying items to move Edwards with the least chance of doing any more damage. They tied the long poles to the back of one of the Indian ponies and four of the Rangers lifted Edwards onto the buffalo skins to soften the trip in the travois. Then Rangers Meijers, Bailey and Cooper escorted Jessie and Edwards back to their tent and the medical supplies Jessie knew would help with his wounds. It took more than the four hours, but they were moving slowly so Edwards wouldn't be in too much pain, although he seemed to remain unconscious since the beating.

Once at the little camp by the stream, Jessie took over ordering the Rangers to place Edwards inside the tent by pulling his dead weight still on the buffalo hide. Jessie thought it would keep the grounds' cold and damp from coming up though the rugs she had brought. Getting the medical supplies, she focused on making up a mixture of garlic, ginger and an herb she knew was an analgesic from the Amazon River basin. She applied the mixture to each open wound and then laid torn up sheets soaked in vinegar on all the bruises, deciding that having him remain on his back lessened the amount of damaged areas concealed.

Sewing the longer gashes and the holes from the spears brought the bleeding to an end. She wasn't sure where she got the strength, but she needed to know he hadn't died trying to lessen her pain. She believed him when he had explained both their danger and that his death had been decreed from the beginning.

Ranger Meijers offered Jessie a cup of coffee and a plate of canned meat heated over the fire. About to refuse, she realized she needed to be able to care for Edwards over the next few days and thanked him then ate the meal. Most of their food had been taken by the Comanche, but she showed the Rangers where she had hidden some to keep marauding animals from getting it. They added that to the troops' own supplies.

The Rangers were very polite, if a little curious since they could see there had only been the one tent. Jessie was unembarrassed or concerned that she was a single lady in close confines with their nearly naked Captain. Besides, they knew she was the best one to care for him. The one most likely to know how to treat his many injuries. And they were impressed she wasn't in hysterics, as she had every right to be, they explained. A couple of minutes later and the Rangers would have been on a recovery mission instead of a rescue.

They may have been more concerned if they knew she had removed what had been left of his clothing to see to his wounds. His trousers were no protection from the nails and sharp blades the braves had used to subject his entire body to pain and torture. Jessie was sure they

37

meant for the beating to continue and would have even used ways to bring him back to consciousness, if he had had the audacity to pass out.

She washed Edwards, using several pans of warm water, gently stroking every part of his torso as she searched for any injuries or bruising, she might have missed the first time she cleaned the blood and dust off him. She wondered what the scars were that showed horizontal cuttings on his chest. Her biggest curiosity was the geometric patterned tattoos on his calves. This bath was more to convince her he was healing and there didn't seem to be the infections she had first feared. She left only a blanket covering him and slept next to him to share her warmth.

Jessie had bathed in the cold stream, warning the red-cheeked Meijers she would be doing so and to please attend to things on the other side of the camp. She then had the chance to change into clean long underwear and wash her hair, using the warm sun of the day to dry it. She wound it at the back of her head in a neat little bun and felt immensely better, more in charge, more herself.

She stayed in the tent most of the day and all through the night, the Rangers having brought their own tents and bedrolls. It was on the third morning Jessie felt the heavy hand on her hip and a hoarse voice whisper into her ear, "Is this heaven then? Did those savages finally kill me?"

"No, and you have to be careful how you move. You have broken or cracked ribs. I've wrapped two fingers together because they are broken. I put in so many stitches I lost count and your back looks like a woodpecker attacked you." She turned to gaze into his dear bearded face then burst into tears.

"Sh-h-h-h, it's all right, we're both safe. I take it the Rangers found us before the Comanche could finish me off?" He pulled her to him, even though it must have been painful. "I told you they would find you. Were you hurt?" he asked gently.

"No, not like what you think. The Rangers came just as they might have killed you. I was so frightened... I don't want to go through anything like that again." She sobbed into his chest, his hair getting wet from her tears.

"I see they left me my male parts," he said as he pushed them towards her body. "They've been known to castrate their male captives before killing them. I don't suppose I could convince you to help me make sure they're still working properly?"

"Edwards, how can you even tease about such a thing?" She returned to calling him by his last name as they had done before their capture. "You came close to losing more than your man parts, I assure you." She meant to sound firm but didn't try to move out of his arms. She told herself it was because she didn't want to hurt him, but it was because she was exactly where she felt the safest.

"How long have I been lazing around here? I take it there are Rangers just outside?" He laid his lips against her shoulder.

"Um-m-m, there are Meijers, Bailey and Cooper protecting us. The rest of the division took the Comanche to the fort. You've been unconscious for more than forty-eight hours." She stroked the hair that had fallen forward off his brow, being careful not to hurt any of the wounds. "I'm glad you woke up. I was afraid all those head wounds caused severe damage."

"I'll need to speak with Meijers and then would it be too much to ask for some food?"

"I will gladly bring you some food and if all stays as it is, we'll head back to town tomorrow. I want a real doctor to tend you." Sitting up, she arranged her clothing before going outside the tent. She had returned to wearing a shirt and the leather split skirt when she had brought Edwards back after their rescue. It was less offensive, she felt, to the other Rangers then the trousers Edwards had gotten used to seeing on her.

"Ranger Meijers, Edwards is awake and is hungry. A very good sign of recuperation. I'll get something for him, if you would like to speak with him."

Meijers smiled and said gratefully, "Thank you, Dr. Reeves, we are so glad you were here to help him after that beating. He wouldn't have made it home, not in his condition. Do you have any idea when he'll be able to travel?"

"I can hear you, you young pup. Ask me when I'll be able to travel for God's sake. I'm not simple minded, you know," Edwards yelled through the canvas.

Meijers almost jumped to attention then realized Edwards couldn't see him and bent to enter the small tent to get information from his senior officer.

Jessie crawled into the tent and stretched out next to Edwards after the man had sat up part of the day taking his meals with the rest of the Rangers. She watched his face, still unused to his full beard. "How did you know what they were going to do with us? How do you know their language? It can't be an easy one to learn."

Edwards took a deep sigh and then told her quietly, "The woman I told you about, the one who was finally rescued from her Comanche captors, was my mother."

"Oh, Benjamin, how awful for her. I'm so sorry." Jessie was at a loss to express her sorrow for the woman who had given him life.

"My father was a Major in the Rangers and led the division to drive the Comanche onto the reservation when he came across this rogue tribe holding my mother, a very obvious captive. There were several and the Rangers escorted them to the nearest fort, but no one ever came in response to my mother's name being published. She had been a captive for over five years and had a son she wouldn't give up." He allowed her a few seconds to come to grips with his words before continuing.

"Her family might have come for her if there hadn't been a child, but the stigma is always there. The captives are usually raped by all of the warriors and treated as the lowest of humanity, beaten, burned, cut and mutilated. I don't want to go into it. I'm sorry I got carried away for a while just explaining it to you," he apologized and pulled her closer to his chest.

"I'm sorry. I didn't mean to be so intrusive. I was simply curious. You know I never know when to stop questioning anything." She tried to let him know he didn't owe her any answers.

"It isn't a big secret, though, as time goes by most of our neighbors don't think about it any longer. She's merely the wife of Major Edwards, retired. To me, she's always simply been my mother. I never knew her before so I don't know if being a captive for so long changed her or not." As he thought for a moment, he finished, "It would have had to though. No gentle woman could live through what she had, see what she saw and not have it change her in so many ways."

"But your father, he loved her or did he merely feel sorry for her and take her in?" Jessie thought possibly she had stepped beyond what Edwards was ready to talk about.

"My father adores her, for him she walks on water. I guess he has been that way ever since first setting eyes on her among the squaws as they rounded them up to march them to Indian Territory. He says their gazes met and he walked right up to her and asked her if she knew her real name. She did although it was hard for her to speak in English after so many years. He took her up on his horse and another Ranger took the boy, kicking and cursing onto his and they rode back to the fort with them." Edwards laughed. "Love at first sight they call it."

"That is a kind of love story. At least she finally found the right man, the one she was made for. But what happened with the boy?" The anthropologist in her needed to know.

"He tried living with the Major and his mother, but couldn't take the insults to his mother and himself. Couldn't make it in school without fighting, spoke broken English, and looked too Comanche to make it easily in the Whiteman's world. He left his mother and returned to the Comanche on the reservation where he lived among them until he was an adult." Edwards was unemotional.

"I'm sorry about that. It had to be difficult to be raised one culture and try to live in another, no matter how supportive the people around you are. And these two cultures are worlds apart from what I saw. I have never been involved in such a barbaric tribe as that and I never want to again."

"You will never have to again. We'll head back to town where you can relax and have a real hot water bath and a fine dinner with wine," he told her, spinning dreams of good things in her head as she fell asleep in his arms.

There was no fanfare when the travel weary group arrived in town, going directly to the Ranger's camp and getting Edwards settled in his tent. They sent for the doctor, although Edwards said he had been wounded enough in the past to know he was fine and healing as well as can be expected. The doctor came and confirmed that opinion before Jessie rode her horse to the hotel where she had left her city clothes and checked in, asking about a hot bath as she did.

The hotel was modest in comparison to eastern hotels, with its stenciled walls in the lobby and potted plants. The carved wood framed furniture with firm damask covered seats was similar to many Chicago hotel foyers and public rooms. Several high, turtle shaped marble tables with colored glass oil lamps were set about the room and to the side was a check in desk where the same clerk stood who was on duty when Jessie left almost three weeks earlier.

Her room was a welcome oasis with its large soft bed, lace curtains and pulldown shade to block out the bright Texas sun. The clerk had told her he would have her trunk brought up to her room and she sat in the chair next to a table and opened the satchel she had brought upstairs with her. Taking out the sketch pad and note book, she paged through it, seemingly weeks had gone by since she glimpsed the neatly printed notes and dainty accurate drawings, but it had merely been a few days. These would be a good basis for the next person taking inventory to use. Jessie would copy these and send the originals to the Smithsonian for safe keeping.

She also fingered the pages full of pencil sketches of her camping companion, before his injuries. Sitting by the evening fire with a half-smoked cigarette or washing-up at the edge of the river. One of him brushing down their cantankerous pack mule, both males showing an attitude. She smiled at those times when she had caught Edwards just being Edwards. But even as she drew them, she knew they would need to part. His life and job were here in Texas, whereas hers was not. She had no one place to live or be. Her career, her way of life is nomadic even more so than the Plains' Indians. She would travel the world, study all climates and visit all sorts of people. She couldn't tie herself to a man tied to one area, even one as large as Texas.

Once clean and dressed in her city clothes as Edwards would have called them, Jessie went down to the dining room and had a full four course meal and felt decadent ordering a chocolate dessert. She didn't imbibe in wine, so felt justified until she wondered what Edwards had had for dinner. Probably nothing as fine as this, but then thought he could have sent someone into town to get the same thing she had eaten if he had wanted to.

Jessie slept fitfully, anxiety and outright fear playing havoc with her dreams or, rather, nightmares. Comanche raiding parties attacking Edwards and her, unable to out run them, unable to save each other. She woke up with tears running down her face and her legs strangled by the twisted sheet. Flipping back and forth under the clean sheets and warm blankets, she worried about how Edwards was doing.

The morning found Jessie ordering breakfast for herself and one to be packed up to go. She asked where she could find a buggy to rent and was soon on her way out to the Ranger's camp a couple of miles outside of town.

She found Edwards sitting up and nursing a cup of coffee. "Yell at me or something, will you? The guys around here are trying to treat me like an invalid." He met her with his complaint as soon as she entered the tent.

"You are an invalid and you should only be sitting up part of the day. Those ribs need to rest and not have weight placed on them from standing and sitting up. Here, I brought you a nice breakfast from the hotel. It's steak and eggs with fried potatoes." Placing the covered plate in front of him, she let the smell of the still hot food tempt his appetite.

"I had breakfast but nothing like this. Sow belly and grits, so I think I still have room." He pulled out a fork and knife from the desk drawer and began to cut into the steak. "Tastes great, but I have a few loose teeth that I'm hoping not to lose so I have to chew carefully."

"I figured you could do with some real food. Not that what the Ranger's cooked wasn't good, merely sort of bland and nothing fresh. Humans need fruits and vegetables, 'man does not live by bread alone' although those tortillas were pretty good wrapped around all those other things."

"My family is coming and taking me back to the ranch to finish my recuperation. Will you stay and meet them? Maybe come back with me for a while?" he asked as he finished the meal in record time.

"I'm due to give several lectures once I get back to Washington. My uncle and aunt are in Austin right now waiting for me and then he will rent a Pullman for us to travel to Washington together. I was only here because the Senate was in recess, but it's due to start up again, too." She regretted having to miss meeting his mother. For some reason feeling close to the woman who had overcome the obstacles, escaped the Comanche, and could live among her own people again.

"I understand you probably want to get as far away from Texas as you can. It can't hold pleasant memories for you." He gazed into her eyes, as if waiting for a denial which she couldn't honestly give him. "If there are consequences of our being together, if you need me at any time, I'll come to you. Here is my family's address and they can get a letter to me. They'll always know where to find me. Do you understand? Any time." He wrote out an address on a sheet of paper and handed it to her.

"There won't be any repercussions, I've started, ah, I'm quite sure of it, but I appreciate your concern. I almost forgot all about it," she fabricated as she picked up her gloves and the empty plate to return to the hotel.

The expression that passed over Edwards' face was difficult to read, but Jessie smiled and leaned down to kiss his cheek. "I'll always be grateful for what you did for me. I know I can always trust the Rangers."

She left while Edwards felt impotent to do anything to stop her. He wasn't even in shape to protect her. He would need to get his strength back and follow her or find her wherever she went in the world. He didn't want this to be the end for them. Certainly not without him able to speak privately or worrying about who was outside the tent.

If he hadn't shown his emotions sooner, it was due to having been on the job, protecting Jessie and anything personal had to wait until he was taken off the assignment. Now wasn't the time, not now when he got tired walking to the latrine, not now when he had a strange ache in his chest merely thinking of her returning to Washington.

CHAPTER FOUR

Jessie fit right back into her social world. Not that she went out in the evenings much, but she was often asked to consult with other scientists, botanists and naturalists - anyone with an 'ists' to the end of their title. She also had a lecture series about her trip to the Himalayas with her father and the diverse plants and climate found there. How they affected the native peoples, their food source, their clothes and choice of fabrics and dwellings. All linked together, using the best and most valuable commodity for each aspect of their culture, their world.

The trip to Texas was shelved far into the back of her memories. When she thought of Texas, she only wanted to remember her meeting Edwards and maybe their after-dinner arguments sometimes referred to as conversations. She would know when it was safe to do so. When she stopped waking up in the middle of the nights sweating and sobbing, not remembering what had brought her to such a state but knowing its origin.

Purposely pushing all thoughts of that man and time out of her mind, she focused on the plans for her next research. It seems the trip to Texas had sealed her place in the academic world of anthropology. Although not actually working in her field, the university was allowing her to organize and oversee a trip to study the shoreline of Florida. It was something she had wondered about and this would give her the opportunity to do so without funding the expedition herself. How indigenous people and those arriving by Spanish galleon could have altered the original natural plants and animal life associated with them. Someone else, a male, was doing a similar study where there had been a Spanish colony for decades. The two would be compared by yet others taking into consideration the difference in locations.

Preparing for a study, setting up the travel plans and making a list of provisions and supplies that would be needed for the length of the expedition would be time consuming. She could hide from reality for weeks and that wouldn't even include the travel time.

Jessie was cutting the dead branches off the rose bushes before snow set in, what snow they would get in the Washington D. C. area, anyway, when she glanced up to see what she first thought was a mirage. A tall man dressed in a black suit with grey print waistcoat, white shirt and black tie, polished black city boots and a top hat in his hand stood in the shade of her uncle's house. The face wasn't unknown to her, although the beard had been shaved, the soft mustache was still in place.

Jessie swayed with the shock of seeing him before catching herself saying, a smile in her voice, "Why Ranger Edwards, how nice of you to drop by. May I offer you something to drink?"

"Your uncle and aunt already have, thank you. He said it would be all right for me to come out here to speak with you. You're not too busy, are you?" He sounded stilted, not like the man across the campfire from her.

"No, not busy, but you must excuse my apron and work gloves. I love to work outside with the plants and it was such a nice day." She held herself back from asking outright why he was there, but then again, she was dying to know what had brought him all the way from Texas.

"I wanted to let you know I resigned from the Rangers, letting the eager younger men have my place." She noticed his nervousness as he turned his hat around and around in his hands.

"Not because of what happened to us, was it?" she asked, worried his wounds might have been worse than she thought or the beating had affected his ability mentally.

"No, it had been in the works before we even met. I had given up my rank to another man who was making the Rangers a career. I never planned on doing so and actually stayed longer than I had first thought. I wanted to put in my time as a way of letting my father know I respected his choice and for my mother by rescuing other Comanche captives." He walked closer, his raspy voice music to her ears.

"I see. I didn't know. I guess it never came up," she said, still unsure of why he was here, what he knew or thought he knew.

"I'm pretty much healed, although the ribs still give me fits if I try to do too much in one day. The salves and tincture you left really helped." He stopped moving and then asked, "May I smoke? I'm feeling a real need to do so right now."

"Certainly, you know I've always liked the smell of tobacco." She hoped the aroma of his special tobacco wouldn't bring back the evenings they spent together talking and getting to know one another.

As soon as he lit the cigarette and blew the plume of smoke up into the grey sky, as soon as Jessie got a whiff of the fragrant odor, she became faint, turned quickly, bending over the thorny bushes emptying her stomach contents all over them.

Edwards immediately dropped his cigarette and came up behind her, holding her in case she fainted as he must have thought she was going to do. "Are you ill? You should have told me. You shouldn't be out here with these damn plants. They can take care of themselves. Should I call for your aunt?"

Wiping her mouth with the bottom of her gardening apron, she waved him away. "No, she doesn't know," Jessie said, trying to make herself presentable, trying not to dry heave into the same bushes as before and trying not to alarm her aunt, who would put two and two together soon enough.

"Doesn't know what, Jessie? That you're ill?" He seemed legitimately confused, which gave her hope she could still get away with her plan.

"Let me sit over here. There's a bench. I simply need to sit and don't light another cigarette, I implore you." She rested her head on her hands, inhaling deeply of the fresh cool air.

Edwards stood seemingly helpless as Jessie began to get the color back into her face and she smiled up at him. "I knew it would pass in a couple of minutes. Just a female thing, nothing to worry about, I assure you."

"You're with child," he stated bluntly, somehow knowing without further words. "My child, and you were going to hide that information from me? Were you thinking of getting rid of it?" His rough voice sounded condemning and hung in the air between them.

She was angry at him for bringing the need to explain herself to anyone so soon. "If I was going to get rid of it, I wouldn't be throwing up my dinner in the bushes. I simply haven't decided the best way to tell people."

Edwards seemed to be holding his temper in check. "I suggest we announce it a few months after our marriage."

"I can't marry you, Edwards. We did what we did because I begged you and I am still grateful. You eased my mind when my world was spinning out of control and I thought life as I knew it would be over. I do not want you to feel obligated in any sense, here. I can financially afford this child and I will work out a believable story and raise him or her as I was raised."

"But what about me? Am I to simply forget I have a child somewhere, living who knows where? I don't think I can agree to that. We will have to come to some other arrangement." He paced in front of her. "You must recognize that I'm part of the equation, now I know. You and I are irrevocably joined."

"I'll let you know whether it's a boy or girl. You can visit, but I can't give you more than that." She couldn't look into his eyes to see the recrimination she knew would be there.

"No, Jessie, we'll need to do better than that or I'll go into that house and tell your uncle you and I spent weeks in a single tent together and now you are having my child." She knew he was trying to force her hand.

"Don't, please, don't do that. He controls my money for another couple of years, even the money I make on my books and lectures. I won't be able to live if you turn him against me." The tears in her eyes started to roll down her cheeks and splash onto the apron.

Edwards sat next to her on the bench and took one hand, rubbing it with his thumb. "I'm sorry I said that. No matter what happens I'll support you and the child. Never worry about being alone, all of my family will be there for you. I promised not to leave you, remember?"

She stared down at their clasped hands and said so quietly he had to lean closer to hear. "I don't remember much of that day. I don't want to remember it." She hesitated then continued, "I know what we did made me feel, I don't know, cherished, I guess, and I felt stronger afterwards." Shaking her head, she continued, "But I can't think of anything else about that day or I get anxious, almost sick with dread. To realize how close we came to death, to realize I was causing you all that agony."

"Why do you blame yourself? I should have seen that war party. I was there to protect you. If there is blame, lay it at my feet," he told her fiercely.

"I don't think anyone could have seen them. After they captured us another brave came in from more than a mile away with their horses. They must have crawled in on their stomachs all that way not to be seen. We were simply in the wrong place," she told him just as fiercely.

"So, you absolve me of my guilt but hold on to yours like a mantle? What am I to do with you? You need a protector and I want to be that man."

"I have plans, things I want to do with my life."

"Like what? Will you still be able to do them while watching a young child?"

He asked practical questions as she usually did. Only one of the things they had in common, had them talking late into the night around the campfire.

"I'm about to go to Florida to study the plant growth through the winter months and then I was to study the Inuit in the Alaskan Territory, which can best be done in the summer months. But I'll be due to give birth by then so I guess I'll have to cancel. The museum will give the study to someone else," she said quietly as she realized how many of her plans may need to be curtailed with an infant in tow.

"The Seminole have been pretty quiet now, so I don't see a problem with traveling to Florida, if you agree to take the train as far as we can. Depending on where you are planning the study, the weather can be quite pleasant during the winter. By spring we can decide where you wish to have the baby born, but I rule out the middle of the Atlantic right now." He watched her intently. "You can see the sense in my going with you, can't you?"

"Edwards, don't talk foolishness. You have plans, too, even if you don't want to return to the Rangers. I can't let you put your law degree aside for me."

"For you and my child, then. I can't have you go traipsing off on your own any more. I'm not leaving you."

She put her free hand to her head where a throbbing was building. "I'll have to think about this, Edwards. I was living one day at a time, trying to get through this without breaking down in tears every few hours."

"I'll dry your eyes for you if you do. This can be overwhelming if we don't stick together. I'll come by tomorrow and we can talk again after you are well-rested."

"I haven't been well-rested since I left you and then there were days before that I can't remember closing my eyes. I've got a lot to think about."

"A wise woman once told me 'don't think about it, just do it' and I'm still glad I took her advice." He kissed her forehead as he stood helping her to her feet.

Jessie's cheeks felt flushed as she remembered when she told him that right before they made love. Perhaps she did remember more of that day than she thought.

Jessie dressed in her city clothes for the lectures and debates she was asked to attend. She had to appear capable and feminine. The fashionable bustle was covered with yards of extra cloth, trimmed with colored ribbon and tied up into swages with several bows. She wore a hat that was a completely winsome concoction made to arrest the male eye and bring them to their knees, but Jessie wasn't interested in the many kind gentlemen who surrounded her after her lecture. She smiled and accepted their praise and cards. She remained untouched in the heart, even though several of the men seemed more than interested in her as a female, not merely a female anthropologist.

She turned as the mostly male crowd separated and Edwards came forward, taking her arm and giving her a light kiss on her cheek, settling the unasked questions among the other men as they disseminated quietly leaving Edwards the floor.

"Why did you do that, Edwards? I was simply answering some additional questions. These attendees are who buy my books and that is how I make my money to continue my research," she explained as he escorted her towards her cape and reticule then helped her on with both.

"I came to take you to tea. You seemed a little pale to me, but now you seem to have color. You haven't developed an abhorrence of tea and sweets, have you? Like the smell of tobacco?" He guided her onto the street, checking both ways before crossing to a coffee shop.

"I can't seem to tolerate the smell of coffee early in the morning."

Edwards searched the almost empty shop worriedly as she continued, "But don't worry, it seems to only be first thing in the morning. I've been avoiding the breakfast room until my uncle leaves. My aunt prefers tea, as do I, so we sit and drink a pot together after Uncle goes in to the Senate floor. I'm lucky he likes to start early with his mail and constituents." She settled herself across the small table from Edwards so she could admire him in his town clothes.

He placed their order. "What kind of a look is that you're giving me? Do I have smut on my nose or something?"

"No, yesterday I was so surprised at seeing you I didn't really look at you, if you know what I mean. You are an extremely handsome man and the beating you took didn't harm your appearance in the least. Even the scar hiding in your hairline makes you seem dashing. I never thought of you fitting into civilian life you made such a handsome, rugged Ranger." She finished her inspection, noticing his cheeks in full blush.

He almost laughed. "How can I argue with that? I'm quite the catch I've been told. Of course, my mother was the one telling me so I did take it with a grain of salt.

Want to throw your hat over the windmill and take me on? I promise to be housebroken before you know it."

Jessie knew there was a real question there, but was saved from answering when their meal was served and she took up the duties of hostess and poured for them both. The conversation for the rest of the meal was along the lighter side. Questions an attendee to one of her lectures might have asked her. Nothing to strain the fragile bond that was forming between them. Nothing to remind her of that day she didn't want to remember but could never forget.

After more than an hour, Jessie apologized. "I really must be getting home or my aunt will begin to worry. I usually go right home after an assembly or lecture. This was very pleasant, though, and I thank you. I will need to remember the cream cakes here are well worth traveling across town to order."

"The pleasure today was all mine, I assure you," he said in return, almost as the polite strangers they were pretending to be. "I'll hail a cab for you."

As they were leaving the shop, a tall, dark skinned man held the door for them and she felt Edwards tense next to her as she glanced into the face of the stranger who seemed familiar at the same time. Sweat beaded on her forehead and back of her neck, she stopped in her tracks, unable to take a step forward, to come any nearer to this man. He had his long black hair pulled back at his neck with a colored piece of cloth holding it in place. His black eyes seem to rake over Jessie and then stare directly into Edwards' gaze.

"Morgan," said a terse Edwards, nodding in acknowledgement of the courtesy done by the stranger, no not stranger, Edwards knew this man, this Indian.

Jessie relaxed a little, knowing Edwards was on speaking terms and finished walking past and onto the brick sidewalk.

The stranger, dressed as a gentleman in suit, shirt and tie, and wearing a stovepipe hat, nodded in return and responded, "Edwards." Then disappeared into the coffee shop, leaving a shaken Jessie and an obviously angry Edwards by the edge of the street.

Edwards was quiet as they waited for the cabbie, he hailed to bring the buggy up to the curb where they stood. He smiled and said, "I'll come by tomorrow, I have some things to take care of today."

Jessie nodded her understanding and watched as the cab pulled away. She thought she saw Edwards turn and enter the coffee shop again just as the cab rounded the corner.

Jessie had a fitful, dream filled night. A dark eyed granite faced stranger, no, again not a complete stranger, but the man who confronted them at the coffee house, appearing whenever Jessie was least expecting him. She woke groggy and decided she would rather be awake than face any more anxiety filled moments trying to sleep. Besides, she had another lecture that day and she couldn't drink the reviving cup of coffee she usually would take after a bad night like she had just had.

Jessie was feeling back to her old self by the time the lecture ended. She enjoyed relaying her knowledge to people who were interested in the same subjects she was, even if they didn't always agree with her findings. The Bible was often touted as a scientific chronicle and anything she said to the contrary of its teachings were often attacked. She had gotten used to those people and didn't hold their beliefs against them, but she surely wasn't about to agree with them. There was too much physical proof of prehistoric animals and ape-like man to ignore Darwin completely, although she didn't swear by everything he wrote or thought, either.

It was at the end of the lecture when Jessie was usually surrounded by people who wanted her to sign their books or the program from the lecture when a lovely older lady approached her. Jessie again got the feeling of familiarity and smiled as she came to the end of her admirers and the woman was still waiting for a moment of Jessie's time.

"I'm so glad you were able to attend the lecture. I hope I was able to excite your interest in anthropology and the world around us." Jessie repeated the same refrain she told all the people who wished to speak with her but didn't seem to have any questions.

In a well-modulated voice, the woman responded, "I'm more interested in you, my dear. I am Benjamin's mother, Emily Edwards."

Jessie knew her mouth dropped open. This fashionable woman with her premature white hair wrapped elaborately into a French twist and topped with the most stunning hat Jessie had seen this side of Paris was the woman who had found a new life. The lady wore a dress of deep maroon and black lace, a row of black onyx buttons from the high collar down to the waist and at the tight cuffs. Black gloves and beaded reticule swinging from her wrist simply did not match with the woman Jessie knew had been a captive of the Comanche tribe for over five years.

Jessie hopefully collected herself enough to reply politely. "Oh, Mrs. Edwards, how nice to meet you.

Ranger Edwards had wanted us to meet while I was still in Texas, but I had to return to Washington with my aunt and uncle." Then added, so the woman wouldn't think meeting her was of less importance than traveling, "I was contracted to do these lectures and had already received payments for them. I couldn't reschedule the rooms for months."

"That is quite all right, dear. Do you have time for a coffee or tea?" The pleasant woman tilted her head slightly like a little bird.

Jessie smiled and then acquiesced. "There's a very nice place across the street that has the best cream cakes and I've been thinking about them all morning."

Once seated at the same table she had been at with Edwards, both women removed their gloves after placing their order. Jessie waited for the other lady to speak first since she evidently had something to say to her.

"I wanted to thank you personally for taking such good care of my son when he was injured," Mrs. Edwards began. Jessie interrupted her immediately, not wanting to be thanked for saving the man who had been hurt protecting her. He wouldn't have even been in the desert in the way of those Indian renegades, if she hadn't wanted to draw plants.

"Really, please don't thank me. I owe my life to your son. He could have died trying to save me. I will forever be grateful and in his debt. I still feel a great obligation to him."

"But nothing more? Nothing besides gratitude?" Mrs. Edwards seemed concerned, her brows brought down in worry lines. The action so reminiscent of her son.

"I, I don't know what else there could be? I hold him in the highest regard. He is noble and brave and loyal to a fault. I was blessed to have met him and to think of him as a friend." Jessie was now confused with what the other woman wanted her to say. "What has brought you to town, Mrs. Edwards? Did you travel with Ranger Edwards?"

"No, I wasn't sure where he went when he left me at the ranch. He said he was well enough to travel and left. My sons are both very independent of their father and me. Of course, they are old enough to know what they want. I actually travelled with my oldest son," she said as if it were the most common thing in the world to travel with the child who was a product of rape.

The waiter brought their order and placed the items onto the table while the two women remained quiet, both thinking what to say next to make this awkward meeting go better.

Mrs. Edwards did the pouring and as Jessie played with her cup the older woman finally blurted out, "I know how frightened you were when the Comanche took you and I know you turned to Benjamin to save you. It is natural. The Comanche are fearsome devils and cannot be trusted around innocents and civilized men. I know this to my own sorrow and so does Benjamin. He has had to endure their vicious assaults twice now and both times was saved and brought back to life." She turned for some response from Jessie.

The cup rattled on the saucer and Jessie took her hands off it. "Despite the Rangers that came to our rescue, I believe it was Ranger Edwards who saved me. I, in turn, made sure he got the medical care he needed and I could provide. But what do you mean twice? How was he saved the first time? He told me they let him go."

"No, my oldest son, his brother Morgan, saved him the first time." Jessie felt dizzy hearing the name again, but Mrs. Edwards continued, "He made them put Benjamin through the trials to become a warrior rather than torture him to death, although some would say it was much the same thing. The requirements to become a Comanche warrior are very stringent, very rigorous and Benjamin had already been tortured for several hours when Morgan came back into camp to find his younger brother stretched out between four horses."

Jessie's mind was going a mile a minute, racing back to the face of the dark-skinned man who held the door open for them. The cold way each spoke to the other. It began to make more sense now. Edwards would resent his brother yet owe his life to him at the same time. It wouldn't make for a merry time around the family dinner table.

"So, the old scars, the ones that looked like slices into his chest, they were from the torture?" Jessie asked, getting sick thinking of the pain Edwards had endured.

"No, those were from the trials given to the warriors. Morgan has the same ones." As the older woman must have realized this is not where she wanted the conversation to go added, "My youngest son holds you in the highest esteem. I hope you are not dissuading him because of me, of my circumstances with the Comanche." There the fear was out, the question asked but not demanding an answer.

Jessie felt sorrow that this lovely woman would think Jessie would hold something like her captivity against her or her son. "Oh, no, never. It's simply that I don't think Edwards, Benjamin, is really thinking things through. He still feels protective of me, but he doesn't owe me anything. I'll be fine." She patted the older lady's hand across the table, noticing for the first time the scars and dark marks covering it.

Mrs. Edwards grimaced. "The battle scars of war, my dear. At least you were spared these. The squaws are very jealous and very vindictive. I was given as a gift to the war chief because he had recently lost a wife in childbirth. I was to bear him healthy children and the medicine man blessed our union. The squaws were not pleased, of course, and their way was to cut and burn and mistreat the captives, sometimes maiming them beyond recognition." Mrs. Edwards gazed out through the front window, remembering a past time, a past life she would never forget and never miss.

"I was one of the lucky ones because one of the older squaws took a particular dislike of me. She had wanted her granddaughter to be the chief's new wife. One day she cut off one of my ears saying I wasn't listening to her properly. My husband, I mean the chief, was not pleased and had her right hand cut off as punishment."

Jessie had to close her eyes, trying not to stare at Mrs. Edwards missing ear hidden behind her hair and not visualize the apt punishment dealt out to her abuser. Her stomach rolled again and all thoughts of tea fled.

"I'm not telling you these things to frighten you or to make you feel sorry for me. After that incident the cutting and burning lessened. I was pregnant with Morgan and as newer captives came in the squaws forgot about me and I was accepted into the tribe as the war chief's main wife. Not another brave even glanced at me.

I held a position of importance since he was a very popular chief and I was the bearer of his first-born son."

Jessie lost all interest in the tea and cream cakes. In fact, she may never be able to enter this coffee shop again. She unconsciously placed her hands over her abdomen saying a prayer of gratitude that this child had not been a result of rape. That it was wanted and loved, that she wanted it and loved it even this early.

Mrs. Edwards, studying Jessie said, "Benjamin assured me you were not assaulted, that you were rescued before the Comanche could touch you." She hesitated then continued, "But you are with child, I can see that now. And Benjamin is the father. I should have realized he was too agitated these last few days for it to simply be that you turned down his proposal."

Jessie tried to find a way to take back the words, for her condition to stay a secret a little longer so she could rethink her plans. Make some decisions without worrying her uncle would send her from the house. "What proposal? Edwards didn't mention a proposition, he said he had to think on the plan. I haven't agreed to anything, yet." She noted how relaxed the older woman appeared now that the child was acknowledged.

"Benjamin didn't tell me where he was going, but he did ask for his Grandmother Edwards' rings that I was holding for him until he needed them for his bride. I am very sure you were supposed to be that bride. I don't know where things changed, but I was hoping when I met you, I could help you understand. I thought you were telling him no because of me. But you have totally different reasons and I am at a loss as to how to help either of you." The woman seemed completely perplexed.

Suddenly Edwards was in the coffee shop striding towards the two women in his life who he loved. Bending he kissed his mother. "Mother, I thought we were going to wait until I brought Jessie for a visit." Then he bent and kissed Jessie on the cheek as well.

Edwards sat his large body on the remaining chair at the table and signaled for another cup from the hovering waiter who saw him arrive and remembered the large gratuity from his tea the day before. He eyed the still full tea cups and the untouched cream cakes and firmed his lips. This was going to be more difficult than he thought.

Reaching over, he clasped Jessie's hand lying on the table beside her cup. "Is there anything I can do to make things better for you, easier?"

Jessie's lips began to tremble and he thought for sure she was going to break out in sobs. He patted her hand and then began a simple conversation with his mother, letting Jessie regain her composure.

"Mother, I made a visit to the Senate and spoke with Coronel Bailey. He wanted to know how his son was doing and I told him. He's a little immature right now although I didn't say that to his father, of course. We were all raw recruits at one time and he doesn't have many years under his belt, yet. I also stopped by and met with my uncle, he passes on his greetings to you and father and invited us back for Christmas if we want to spend it in the cold and snow." He couldn't keep his gaze from going over to check that Jessie appeared less pale and worried.

"Don't tell me you ladies are slimming or some nonsense, try these cream cakes mother, they really are very good." He lifted the plate toward his mother.

She played along and took one and placed it on the

small plate in front of her. "Yes, Jessie told me they were exceptional. Perhaps we should take some back to our hotel."

Jessie finally lifted the cup of now cold tea and drank some, her stomach less queasy than it was only moments before. She smiled as mother and son talked, nodded as if she were paying attention, waiting for a lull in the conversation so she could take her leave, make her escape. She was brought out of her reverie when Edwards asked her a question and she hadn't heard it.

"I'm sorry. I was thinking I need to get home before my aunt worries. I'm never late for dinner." Then laughed. "Although I don't take tea so late usually, either." She stood then gathered her cape and gloves. "Thank you so much, Mrs. Edwards. I was delighted to meet you."

"I'll hail a cab and ride home with you. You don't seem all that well, yet," Benjamin told Jessie solicitously as he stood and helped his mother with her coat.

That's all it would take to then need to explain why this man was hanging around after her having to explain away his visit the other night. Jessie felt her face flush after only moments ago getting done telling his mother there wasn't anything between them. For him to waltz in and kiss her in public was beyond the pale. If anyone was around who knew her uncle, she was in for more difficult times that evening at home.

"No, thank you, I've been hailing my own cab for years. Don't worry about me. I'm quite able to take care of myself." She didn't wait for Edwards to pay the bill, but left in a hurry making sure there were no dark strangers lurking by the door.

Jessie spent another horrible night after telling her aunt she was too full from the late tea she had eaten and went right to her room which wasn't unusual. Jessie often spent the evenings rewriting her notes or putting color to her drawings. She did neither this evening, suffering through nightmares again. This time of having to watch Edwards being tortured, of dark-eyed men slicing through his skin and laughing as he writhed in pain. By the morning she was feverish and then had dry heaves until she was ready to cry with the whole situation.

When her aunt heard about the ailment, that kind lady tut-tutted and then told her the best thing would be to sleep the rest of the day. She told her aunt it must have been something bad in the cream cakes and she would never eat at that coffee shop again.

Jessie did sleep a little during the day, the daylight chasing the worse of the nightmares away. The queasy stomach persisted, though. Why in the world was it called morning sickness if it plagued one all day and night? Jessie was just falling asleep again when her aunt knocked on the door and stepped in.

"That nice Mr. Edwards just stopped by to see you. He had brought some of those nasty cream cakes that made you so ill and I told him so. He seemed mortified he had brought more of them since he was under the impression you liked them. He said he will try to return tomorrow, hoping you will be better by then." The woman made sure there was water in the pitcher and patted down the bed cover. "He's ever so handsome. You never said you had tea with him." She fluffed the pillows trying to make her niece more comfortable.

"I had tea with his mother. He came to escort her home as I was leaving," Jessie fabricated to prevent her aunt from becoming suspicious about the two of them.

"See, just as I thought, a fine young man who takes care of his mother. You could do worse than a nice young man like him." Her aunt thought no woman could be content unless she was married.

"You know my opinion on that. No man would allow me the freedom I need to continue with my work and I'm still young enough to want to do field work. I may be going back to Europe after this trip to Florida," Jessie told her aunt as she was leaving, laying the ground work to remove herself from a society that knew she was an unmarried woman.

"Well at least there aren't any wild Indians in Europe. Only groping Frenchmen," her aunt warned as she left her niece in peace.

Jessie lay back thankfully in the bed and prayed for the malaise that seemed to be worse than ever before to lessen. She would need to finish two more lectures before she could make her escape out of the capital. Her aunt wasn't going to be fooled for much longer if the baby insisted on making Jessie so ill.

However, it was as worrisome Edwards was still in D. C. and not heading back to Texas. Moreover, what had his mother meant by telling her he had asked for his grandmother's rings? There must have been some other reason since Edwards hadn't even been aware of the pregnancy. Mrs. Edwards must have misspoken and she had been asked for the rings here in Washington.

The next day Jessie felt well enough to give the lecture and returned home immediately afterward, feeling more tired than usual, wanting to sleep for a couple of hours before dinner. That's when her aunt reminded her they were all scheduled to attend a musical evening at another prominent Senator's home followed by dancing and refreshments. Jessie couldn't tell her aunt she was ill again so soon and with no cream cakes to blame, so she took a short nap and then got ready to go to the evening event.

Jessie felt overly warm in the room that was being used for the dancing. The soprano who had entertained them earlier in the evening was passable, but opera had never been Jessie's favorite. She was hoping to find a quiet room somewhere in the house, but didn't want to get too comfortable in case she fell asleep. It would be so embarrassing for her uncle if she were found dozing in the coat closet.

She had been observing the dancers when she felt someone watching her. Turning slightly, she met the dark eyes of Morgan as he walked towards her. Jessie glanced around but found no exit of escape, then turned to face her nemesis when he stopped next to her.

He leaned towards her to be heard over the music. "I hear congratulations are in order."

Jessie was surprised he knew about the baby and put her hands protectively over her stomach, the memory of how the Comanche killed babies, sometimes cutting them out of the mothers' womb racing through her mind.

His eyes narrowed at her movement and then he tilted his head. "That explains a lot, Dr. Reeves. Would you do me the honor of dancing with me?" He held his hand out politely and Jessie was afraid to refuse, keeping in mind he was Comanche, that he had left his mother to return to his father's savage ways.

She followed him onto the dance floor as another waltz began taking the first step as naturally has if he had been born dancing. They were surrounded by other dancing couples, some of them peering questioningly at her. But Jessie couldn't control the fear that had almost petrified her when he put his hand on her waist, so close to her child. Would anyone there dare stop him if he pulled out a knife and sliced her open? Would anyone come to her aid if she cried out?

"Dr. Reeves, please relax or you're going to do yourself an injury. I'm afraid you're under a misapprehension. I'm in Washington to bargain for all Indian Tribes to be treated equally under the Federal laws. I am not the savage you imagine me to be or my brother may have told you I was." He spoke softly, leaning down to be closer to her ear.

"He's said nothing about you, other than you went back to the tribe when you had the chance. I don't know why you're doing this to me." She sounded bitter to her own ears, her legs were shaking and a tremor ran through her body.

He narrowed his eyes and if Jessie didn't know better an expression of hurt crossed his features. "I'm sorry, I made an error and possibly this wasn't such a good idea. I merely meant to introduce myself to my new sister-in-law-to-be."

"I'm nothing of the sort. I don't know who would have said such a thing," she said with a brittle smile, trying to keep her composure as he maneuvered them through the crowded dance floor to return her to the spot where she had been standing before.

Then there was another large man in their path. Edwards, his face grim as he glared at his brother. "I'll cut in if you don't mind, Morgan."

Morgan stopped and made a little bow to them both. "Certainly, little brother. A lovely lady, if I may say so." Then he stepped off the dance floor and Edwards took her in his arms as she felt the tenseness leave her body. He practically held her up for the final few moments of the music.

"We need to get you somewhere less public. People are still watching us. You were deathly white. Are you feeling better yet?" His gaze searched for a quiet place.

"Down this hall." She pointed to the room she had decided would be the best place for her to sit out the rest of the night before Morgan asked her to dance, before she felt like her life was over.

Edwards entered the room glancing around, leading Jessie to the sofa where he knelt next to her and chafed her hands, which felt like ice in his. "What happened, what did he say to you?"

Then all the fear and worry and fatigue came out in a large sob followed by tears and more sobs, but nothing she tried to say made any sense to him so he let her cry it out.

"What's going on in here, Mr. Edwards? What have you done to my niece?" Senator Marland asked angrily when he saw Jessie crying, using the handkerchief Edwards had handed her only minutes before.

"Jessie's simply a little overwhelmed after accepting my proposal of marriage, sir. I hope you will give us your blessing." Edward's lied and looked toward Jessie for her to refute what he had just told her uncle.

71

Then the older man broke out in a wide smile. "I knew there must be more to your visit than merely to talk to someone who you were with a couple of weeks before." He turned toward his niece and added, "And you, Jessie, I knew you've been unhappy since you got back, so now we know why. I'm glad your young man had more gumption and chased you clear across the country. Maybe he can get you to settle down, get a couple of babies on you." He laughed at his own joke.

Edwards had hold of Jessie's shoulder when he stood. He felt her relax so he relaxed, too. Smiling, he told the uncle, "As soon as she gets herself under control we'll return to the party." Gazing down at Jessie as she gazed up at him, he softened. "I care for her very much, sir. I won't leave her."

If the senator thought that was a strange thing for the young man to say he didn't show it. Jessie knew why Edwards had said it, to remind her of his promise to her when she was at her most vulnerable.

Once the door closed behind the senator, he went down on one knee. "I'm sorry, Jessie, I didn't mean to do it that way, but I didn't want him asking for pistols at dawn. Are you feeling better now? Do I have to go and beat the hell out of Morgan, because it wouldn't take much for me to do so about now."

"It wasn't him, not really. He didn't say anything either. I let my imagination and fear take over and I couldn't stop being petrified." She gazed into his eyes and tried a watery smile, wadding up the hankie beyond all recognition. "At least I didn't break down in front of all those people. What would we have told everyone then? Edwards, I don't think I'm going to get over this fear." She looked at him worriedly. "My whole life, my adult life, is based on me going to these native and aboriginal people and living with them side by side. Eating with them, sleeping in their homes, using their tools and implements as they do. How can I do that and freeze in fear when approached by anyone who isn't the same as I am? Isn't White?"

"It's not unusual. I've seen it after young soldiers come back from a particularly difficult battle or especially after an Indian massacre. Sometimes it lasts for a few weeks and sometimes longer. To us, the torture and atrocities that occur in these raids and afterwards is beyond comprehension. I mean just kill your enemy. That should be enough."

"What am I to do?" she worried, lost in her own thoughts.

"First, we will get down to Florida where I hear the weather is quite nice right now and set up our camp. You will draw and take notes to your heart's content. I will take care of you and the camp and when it's time to move to another campsite we'll begin all over again." He wiped her face clean of all tear marks and handed the handkerchief back. "I don't see going up to Alaska to the Inuit. Is that what you called that group?" At her slow nod he continued, "But maybe the next summer. The baby will be a year old, probably weaned and ready to chase a polar bear or two."

She smiled at his ridiculous plans but she had to ask, "You'd do that for me? Live in a tent and rough it miles from civilization?"

"I've lived in a tent for the past five years and for the most part enjoyed it. Winter and summer, cooking for myself, washing my own clothes. I'm not easily dissuaded," he told her as she stood and let him wrap his arms around her. She put her face up to him and he bent and kissed her on the lips as a pledge.

"We better get out there because if I know my aunt, she's being held back from coming in here by my much-beleaguered uncle. We still need to talk but now is not the time. We need to go out there and show them how happy we are."

Edwards held her arm. "If this isn't what you want, if you're not happy, then we can figure out another way. I just want you and the baby protected and safe. It doesn't matter what will make me happy."

"You deserve to be happy, Edwards."

"Then call me Benjamin again. That will make me very happy." He was smiling as she pulled him by the hand towards the hall and waiting group of people, anxious to see the newly engaged couple.

CHAPTER FIVE

The wedding wasn't immediate, but it was to be held within a matter of days. Jessie finished the last of her scheduled lectures and was packing away the un-sold books she brought to these things. The attendees were her largest source of customers and if they bought from her, she would personalize the book for them. These unsold books would go back to the publisher to be sent out to bookstores and university libraries.

Jessie was busy thinking of all the things she had to order for her trip to Florida, the logistics of getting them there and then figuring out how to get supplies delivered to her work camp. The study was planned for six months so she would be there for the full growing cycle.

Glancing up, she saw a shadow cross the open doorway. She hadn't heard the door open or anyone enter. As her eyes accustomed themselves to the sun light coming in, she made out the shape of a tall man. "Benjamin?" she asked, a smile curving the edges of her mouth up in pleasure.

As the man stepped into the light he said in a deep familiar voice, "No, Dr. Reeves, it's Morgan. I was hoping to talk with you where we can be private and say anything that needs to be said."

Jessie stood behind the table taking some comfort in that fact. Her eyes darted to the exit to the side of her. Morgan put his arms up in surrender, saying with a smile, "Please, I come in peace."

"I know it, but I can't be rational right now so if you stop walking towards me, I think I can keep from running out that door."

"I knew there was more to you than your beauty. I'm glad you can be honest with me and with yourself because I need you to be sensible." As she bristled, he added, "Not that you are not sensible, but you know I did not do anything to harm you, yet you are petrified of me. Of what I represent and I understand that, I do." He kept eye contact and didn't move other than to let his hands drop slowly to his side.

"Go on. Say what you wish to say while I still have control of myself." She spoke evenly. Proud she had her voice under control. Willing him to have his say and move on.

"I don't know how much of our family history you know. Sometimes I think it is best to let it be forgotten. However, you are going to be a part of it now and it is something that will come up at some point. You need to know the truth, not what an outsider will tell you." He seemed relaxed now as if knowing she was willing to listen to him was all he wanted.

"I won't go into my mother's captivity, only that I knew she was treated differently than the other squaws. I always thought it was because she looked so different from the rest of us. I was five when the Rangers raided the village and killed so many of my family but not my mother. After a long amount of talking they put her up on a horse and I ran to save her, trying to hit and kick and bite my way free to save her from the white devils who were taking her from me or so I thought. I found out later she had told Major Edwards she would stay with the other squaws and children if I wasn't taken with her to the fort. I was trying to understand why she was being so docile, not fighting and lashing out as the other squaws had. It was a very confusing time for me." He seemed to be reliving the pain and disillusionment of a five-year-old boy.

The anthropologist in her thought about what he said. "I can see you were devastated to lose your way of life even if you were still with your mother. To be dragged into the world you knew to be at the edge of death. Feeling the hatred aimed at you, feeling the frustration of being denied your way of life, of being too small and weak to make any difference. And the knowledge the rest of your family wasn't coming to save you, to take you back to where you belonged." She said the words without thought. Becoming and feeling what that lost five-year-old had.

"I see why you're so good at studying other cultures. You immerse yourself, even when you are not there. Does that empathy extend to a culture that is based on violence and vengeance?" He watched intently reading the conflict of emotions cross her face as she spoke.

"I think so. I do not find it easy because I think the Comanche ways are so detrimental to their own welfare. They are contributing to their own extinction," she said, thinking if the Comanche continued in the same pattern it would mean their complete demise within a matter of years.

"The Numunuu, my people of the Comanche Nation, were over twenty thousand strong only a few dozen years ago. Then the Whiteman brought us small pox and measles and finally cholera almost decimating us. Now we are a few thousand and the bands are separated by hundreds of miles."

"The diseases weren't on purpose. Aboriginal races are often susceptible to the diseases of another." She spoke automatically.

"Not when the bodies of the dead are placed in and near the water sources or free blankets passed out on the reservations have belonged to the ill."

"They didn't do that did they?" At his silence she bowed her head thinking of how low someone had to sink to kill using the body of a dead child. "I'm sorry, it wasn't fair."

He smiled, but not with humor. "I have it from the best sources, but it wasn't anything the Comanche wouldn't have done if the places were reversed. We have come up with more horrendous tortures and ways to end a life than even the Spanish inquisition."

At that remark Jessie's head shot up and then realized she had been thinking of him as an uneducated savage again. What was worse, was he knew what she had been thinking. Shame came over her because she knew better than to judge an individual by preconceived ideas.

He explained, watching her face as she digested this new information. "I went to university. I'm a licensed attorney. I work for the federal government on Indian Affairs and for the State of Texas on Indian Relocation. I'm familiar with several Christian religions and Judaism, but am not convinced they are any better than my own gods and spirits."

"I did not doubt your intelligence or capability to learn. I underestimated your tenacity to do so against all the odds I know were put in front of you." She smiled, showing for the first time she was beginning to understand this dark eyed, dark skinned man in front of her.

"I fought it with tooth and nail to begin with. My stepfather tried to pave the way for me. He left the Rangers and we went to live on the ranch. Any ranch hand who couldn't handle my mother and I being on the ranch was asked to leave, sometimes with a boot print on their butt if they had dared say anything rude about my mother." He stopped speaking to remember those times. "I think that is when I admired him the most. He loved my mother openly, no one doubted his faithfulness, his commitment to make her life happy after what she had gone through. The first few months with him, my mother couldn't wear foot coverings because the squaws had kept her feet burned so with every step she took she would remember she wasn't one of them, would never belong. If her feet healed, they would cut the scars off and burn her again. She walked in pain for years and I was unaware it wasn't natural. It was all I had ever known." The anger of the adult at that young boy came through loud and clear.

"You were a child and you only knew what had been taught to you. If this was normal in your life then that is what you would accept. Don't expect the child you were to reason like the man you are now. You are the same yet different, hopefully able to categorize the amount of guilt you feel to the amount of control you had. There will be latent feelings of frustration and culpability your whole life, but you have to relieve that child you were of any guilt. He was being true to his culture, to society as he knew it." She felt tears in her eyes for that young child who faced too many adult challenges, too soon.

"I never thought of it like that, but I think my mother did. She said once, she felt she had failed me because she did not teach me of her culture. How to speak English or what the world was like outside the Numunuu tipis, buffalos and horses. It was a change once we went to the ranch. I slept outside on the porch wrapped in a blanket, even during the winter, and spent my time working with the horses. My stepfather bought some unbroken mustangs when I got older, but nothing felt like I really belonged there. And then Ben was born and I realized what having a family really meant."

She imagined the smile on his face was as he remembered that small baby wrapped in a blanket, being held by his father, tenderness and love between the parents.

Needing to know the dynamics of the two brothers, the family over all she asked, "Did you resent him? Did you feel he replaced you in some way?"

"No, never," he said in swift denial. "Dr. Reeves, I admire my stepfather for standing up for what he thought was right. I love my mother and my brother very much. And that's saying something since the Numunuu do not even have a word for love, let alone acknowledge anything like that exists. However, I have come to realize what I feel is real and it has a name, love. I am not ashamed to admit to it. I want my mother and my brother to be happy, to be gloriously happy, and I think you make both of them feel that way."

"I don't know about that, but I think Benjamin is happy with me since I'm carrying his child as you have already guessed. But call me Jessie, after all, I am almost your sister-in-law."

"I was going to offer not to attend the wedding. But if you can see yourself able to stay in the same room with me, I would like to be there beside my mother in place of my stepfather," he explained, smiling in their newly found peace.

"I think…." Before she could finish the sentence, a dark blur came from the front door and slammed into Morgan, taking him down to the floor where Jessie could hear fists hitting face as two men wrestled, equally pitted against each other.

A horse voice yelled, "I told you to stay away from her. You know she's afraid of you and yet you come in here just to torment her." Benjamin, who was on top, pulled back his right arm and let his fist smash into Morgan's jaw. "I warned you away once. Now I'm going to make sure you hear me."

Morgan wasn't holding back, at least he didn't appear to be to Jessie. She ran around the table she had been using as a buffer and tried to grab hold of Morgan's arm as he gave Benjamin a punch to his jaw which slid to his eye.

Jessie, trying to find something to grab hold of to pull the men off each other yelled, "Stop this, this instant. Benjamin, stop this. I'm fine, now stop it."

The two men struggled for dominance and rolled so Benjamin was above his brother, cloth ripped and both men beginning to sweat, beads of water dripping from one to the other as each took the upper position, both landing horrible sounding damage to the other.

Jessie gritted her teeth and again tried to get hold of an arm, yelling for the two men to stop fighting when Benjamin pulled back his arm and smacked Jessie in the chin knocking her backwards to land on her buttocks with an "O-o-o-f-f-f."

The men stopped fighting and stared at the woman sitting on the floor, trying to figure out what happened as both of them shouted, "Jessie!"

Followed by Benjamin's, "Damn it!"

Both men scrambled to where Jessie sat, still somewhat bewildered at how she became to be on the floor and then she said, "If I had known that would get you two off one another, I would have tried it earlier." She smiled at the identical dumb expressions on the men's faces.

Benjamin was the first to move, getting up from his knees and helping Jessie up, asking solicitously, "Are you hurt? Is the baby all right?"

Morgan stood up, too, evidently realizing their bad behavior could have serious consequences. He was the first to apologize even though he wasn't the first to strike a blow. "I'm so sorry, Jessie, I never thought you would try to get between us. Only our mother was ever brave enough to do that."

Jessie allowed them to help her up. "You mean you two fought? I mean physically fought each other before?"

The two men looked at each other, noting the bruising that was already beginning to show and said almost in unison, "We're brothers, of course, we fight."

"Then I hope I'm carrying a girl." She brushed off her skirt, finally realizing the fight must be over and who knows who won and what the win accomplished. "Now look at you two. You're brawling on the floor like two ruffians. Straighten yourselves up before someone comes in here and sees you," she finished, sounding as if she were their mother.

Morgan smirked and leaning over to his brother said, "She called me a ruffian. That's probably the nicest thing I've been called in this town."

"It's nicer than anything I've ever called you," replied Benjamin, trying to figure out how to make his coat sleeve stay up on his shoulder now it had been ripped down the seam.

Jessie examined them after their efforts and shook her head at their appearance. "How nice this is going to look at the wedding, both the groom and his best man will have matching black eyes. You're just lucky your mother probably won't see the two of you before the service."

The two men lowered their gaze. Not in shame, but so they wouldn't look at each other and burst out laughing as they often had as teens after a fight and reprimand from their mother. Jessie had a put-upon air and marched out of the assembly hall, the men behind her carrying the boxes of books.

Benjamin was pleased that his intended and his brother seemed to be at least speaking to one another and she wasn't in tears. He couldn't believe his eyes when he saw Morgan standing so close to Jessie who seemed primed to flee clutching the table between them.

He must have misread the situation, though, since neither ran given the chance. He hoped that by taking Morgan to the ground, Jessie would leave to find an area where she felt safe. He was going to follow her after holding a discussion with his pig-headed brother.

Instead, it seems the two of them were at peace – at least with one another.

If Jessie learned to trust again, she won't think she has to stay away from the indigenous tribes and people she wants so desperately to study. He remembered her saddened expression and the desolation in her voice as she confessed to having so deep of fear for anyone different than herself. It was so opposite of the woman he knew in the desert.

That woman reveled in discomfort and living in whatever culture she found herself. The stories she told about bands of Bedouin and the women in the harems. The people of Nepal and the Himalayans were intriguing. She made him sorry he had wasted so much time in Texas, never going anywhere except northern Mexico, which wasn't much different than southern Texas.

He wasn't sure how raising this child was going to work into her plans or how he was for that matter. He did know he wasn't going to leave her to do it on her own. He made a promise and he would make sure she never suffered because he missed sighting the war party that had attacked them.

The wedding took place quickly using the excuse the groom's mother was returning to Texas and the bride and groom were due to be in Florida in a week's time. It would take that long to get them and their equipment to the southernmost state.

Although Jessie wasn't sure marriage was right for her and Ben, it would be right for their child. The stigma of being a bastard wouldn't follow and taint its entire life. Both parents were involved with its birth and Jessie would make sure there was never any feeling of not being wanted and loved. That did not mean that Jessie wasn't thinking ahead and contemplating the time when she would leave Ben and his protection, give him his freedom to pursue a woman who would be the wife he needed, the one he expected to marry.

That woman would probably be Texan and knowledgeable in ranching, shooting and doing what Texan wives needed to do. Willing to take care of hearth and home while the men folk do what men folk do. That life was so foreign to Jessie she didn't even know what those things were, but was sure she couldn't do them. She could cook over an open fire and knew how to set up a tent in soil baked hard by the sun or in three feet of snow and ice. She could build a raft and make a sail from oiled animal skins. She could make a canteen from the bladder of a sheep and a medicinal salve from garlic and ginger root.

But those things weren't what would be expected from the wife of a lawyer in Austin, which was what Ben's plans were. His time in the Rangers and his cartography were merely boyhood dreams fulfilled. More recently, he had been studying to take the bar, now he was older and felt it time to take his place among his peers.

Jessie would hold up her end of the marriage. She admired Ben and his strength and his noble actions to save her as much as he could when the Comanche took them. She had made prayers and vows then that she would stand behind now. He didn't hesitate to help her through her anguish and she would repay him in kind.

She would make their marriage, while it lasted, everything Ben could want. She liked him as a man and was attracted to him physically. Always had been since meeting him on that dusty street next to the stagecoach office. She knew he would be a good father and be there for their child if she ever wasn't able to care for it.

His bride wore a moss-green dress that brought out the green in her hazel eyes. It had a high bustle with fabric that cascaded down to the floor like a waterfall. The new hat, her only new item, had a short veil that was pulled down as she carried a Prayer book with a silver bow and ribbons hanging.

As groom, he wore a dark morning suit with grey vest, starched shirt, tie and black eye. Evidently the pact between him and Morgan not to look at each other directly was still in place. Not because there was animosity between the brothers, but to keep from laughing when they saw what they had done to one another. He thought they looked much more like brothers than usual.

Their mother gave both of them warning glances throughout the ceremony. But to be honest, Benjamin was paying more attention to Jessie than anyone else in the room, even the minister who was performing the ceremony. He was afraid now that he was getting his heart's desire, she would find a way of escaping him. He worried about it until he heard those precious words, "I now pronounce you man and wife."

The wedding party went back to Jessie's uncle's house where there was a small dinner for both families. No one asked about the black eyes and Jessie's aunt, who had grown close to Jessie the past few years, cried as if she were losing a daughter. Jessie assured her she would make the effort to visit them in Washington whenever she could between travels and then he watched as she promised Benjamin's mother the same thing.

Benjamin and Jessie entered the hotel room he had been staying in while in the capital. He thought she seemed apprehensive. He looked the room over as if for the first time, from Jessie's view. It was as nice as the hotel's foyer had been with painted wood work, papered walls and a chintz flowered fabric hanging from the windows and covering two winged-back chairs next to the coal burning stove. The bed was heavily carved with four posters and had a matching side dresser and wash stand. A desk and chair were between the windows facing the front street. The hotel boasted water closets and bathing rooms on each floor, which made it as modern as possible.

"We never discussed the wedding night," he said as he helped her take off her coat. He had already placed his top hat on the dresser and his coat on the hook by the door. "I'll step out while you change, I know you're tired. It's been an exhausting week."

"It's been an exhausting couple of months, but I'm hoping it will slow down now," she told him easily, seemingly at peace with her decision to marry him. "We will have time on the train and riverboat to work things out. I even think the morning sickness is lessening."

He stood holding the door with one foot in the hall. "I hope so. I hate to see you so ill all because of me."

She looked up from placing her hat next to his. "I will never regret that decision so I hope you never do, either."

"How can I when it brought us back together and produced our child? I just need to be sure I haven't changed your life so much that you can't do what you always planned on doing."

Benjamin came in after a light knock, but Jessie was already in bed, the fluffy comforter pulled up to her neck. He went over to turn out the lamp when Jessie stopped him. "I'd like the lamp left on."

Benjamin's heart made a triple beat, but acquiesced, hanging his coat and vest on a hook but laying his suit pants over the back of the chair. He hadn't worn his long johns and warned Jessie as he slid between the sheets. "I don't usually wear anything when I sleep. I did when we shared a tent for modesty's sake, yours not mine." There was humor in his voice.

"That's fine. Remember I saw all of you when I took care of you. I just want to be able to see how the injuries have healed. I haven't seen you naked for a while." He knew he must have appeared surprised because she laughed after the remark.

Pushing down the comforter and sheet, she inspected him closely, a serious expression on her face as she checked each wound, each scar. Without hesitation, she kissed them, her lips following her hands, her gaze and she was at his waist when a groan or moan came from deep within him.

"Although I like, I really like, what you're doing, I'm not sure I can take your attentions anymore." His harsh voice just a whisper.

"Do they hurt? Did I hurt you?"

"Not exactly, but it gets uncomfortable. If you're trying to tell me this is going to be a real marriage, one where we make love and comfort one another then you should continue. If you want something like we had out in the desert, then please roll over so we can go to sleep."

He prayed for her to choose the right answer, the answer he needed to hear.

Jessie smiled and pushed the comforter down so she could reach the spear wound she knew was there, just above his manhood and gave it a tender kiss.

A loudly hissed, "Sh-h-h-h...." escaped as he pulled her up to his mouth and placed it over hers, kissing her as he had been dreaming of doing since he found her in her uncle's garden. He pressed her to him, her breast covered by the thin linen gown. Untying the yellow ribbon holding the collar closed, he let the gown slide open between them.

Benjamin left her mouth and licked one of the pink tipped breasts, then suckled gently before giving the other breast the same treatment. "This won't hurt the baby will it? I mean, if we continue, the baby will be alright?" He tried to keep his mind aware of her needs.

"The baby will be fine, he's well protected."

He kissed her mouth and then her neck and returned to the nipples still wet from his tongue. She was arching toward him, giving him access to everything.

"I don't want to hurt you, so tell me what you like, what feels good and I'll try to take things slow." He pushed her gently onto her back with her breasts open to his view. Pulling the gown over her head, he kissed her again as she became docile and accommodating to his hands and mouth.

His lips traveled over her body as hers had his. He kissed his way from her neck over both breasts and then her navel, which made her giggle and wiggle and then lower, kissing the mound covered with dark silky hair and sliding his tongue between the folds he found there.

Jessie squeaked in surprise and moved her leg as if she were trying to scramble out of the bed. Benjamin held her tightly in place until she stopped squirming and whispered, "We'll leave that for another time. I'll let you have your modesty for now."

Instead, he brought himself up to suckle a breast as Jessie settled under him again.

Benjamin brought his hand to the warm folds he had just been anointing and slid his hand between her unresisting legs. She wasn't a virgin and knew what was ahead for them.

"I want to make sure this is good for you, too. Is there anything you want, need me to do for you?" He wanted this night to go perfectly.

"I don't know. I can't remember the first time. I just wanted you to do what we did." Benjamin stopped doing everything to absorb this information while she confessed. "I know I felt better afterward, not just that I wouldn't be a virgin when I was taken by the braves but all over somehow."

Benjamin was angry at himself for making Jessie remember that day, but he needed her to open up to him before he could continue loving her.

"Tonight was bound to remind me of that day, our being together like this. I knew it would and I wanted to confront it and get it out in the open, then consign it to the past where it belongs. I simply wish I remembered this part, the only you and me part." She finished with the same expression he thought of as theirs. "Don't leave me."

Benjamin positioned himself between her legs and gently entered her, giving her time to stop him if she needed to, if she felt the darkness of that tipi and the urgency of that day overwhelm their time together this night.

Jessie moaned in contentment once his erection was fully enclosed and they were as close as two people could ever be. Taking a deep breath, he kissed her, imitating with his tongue the motion he was about to commence.

"You all right? No bad memories?" he asked, not wanting this night to be linked with that day any more than it had to be.

"I'm beginning to remember now, us, the not leaving me part," she said, encouraging him with the lift of her hips as she had that first time. That was enough for Ben to relax and enjoy this union. He felt her response to his movements, her breathing increasing, her hands caressing his back and buttocks, pulling him closer as she began to reach the pinnacle she was reaching toward.

"Oh-h-h, Ben-n-n, oh, this is wonderful," she whispered beneath his ear and he couldn't have held back if he had a knife to his neck. He pressed deeply into her with his release.

He took some of his weight off her, knowing she was too spent to realize how heavy he was.

"That was wonderful, just…wonderful." She kissed his chest, which was right above her. "I remember that part now. I remember the good parts now." She hugged him to her body.

"Will you do me a favor?" he asked as he rolled off her, taking her with him. "Will you call me Ben from now on? I find I like the sound of your voice when you say it."

"It's a long way from Ranger Edwards, but I think I can manage. I can't promise it will always be in the same breathless way, though."

"I think I can assure that happens if you give me permission." He pulled the comforter over them both, happy they had cleared the worst obstacle in their marriage safely. Now he would work on the less important ones.

As the daylight began to show itself to the newly married couple, Ben found his body wrapped around Jessie, much as he had during their tent cohabitation. She moved, arching her buttocks into him, making his arousal happier than he remembered it ever being before in the morning. She leaned her head back to accept the kiss he wanted to give her and left the hand covering her breast in place, accepting it as she had some mornings in the tent, enjoying the warmth it provided between the two of them.

"I could get up and stir the stove, add more coal since I think it went out some hours ago," he offered as he buried his head into the hair hanging down her neck.

"No, you're better than a stove, I have proof." She tried to tug the covers over her eyes again.

"I've really missed you. I couldn't sleep once you left Texas. I kept waiting to hear you breathing next to me. I finally got some sleep after I saw you in your uncle's garden, but I think last night was the best sleep I've had for some time."

"Me, too, but I think the generous activities you performed had something to do with your good night's rest," she mumbled, ignoring his nudging male member.

He pressed against her in uncontrollable need. She finally moved her leg to accommodate him. He thought this was something he had to get out of his system, but with a little coaxing on his part he made Jessie realized this position could be as satisfying as the other. She finished her orgasm just before he reached his climax and then settled immediately into sleep with her.

When they finally woke up, the sun was high in the sky. The couple got out of bed, each on their side and reached for their clothes, Ben less modestly than Jessie.

"I'm glad we're taking a late afternoon train or this could have become embarrassing. Isn't Morgan picking us up here?" She sounded like a wife to him and his heart lightened. He helped her get into her travel dress without the bustle and corset, which she told him yesterday she wasn't going to wear any longer, no matter what city dress required.

"Morgan can mind his own damn business. I'll sleep with my wife whenever I want to." Then looking over at her added, "Whenever she allows me." He laughed at her expression of consternation, but was so glad she wanted to make this marriage real.

The trip was going to be made in style in a private car, although Jessie's uncle always had a Pullman when making the long trip between the Capital and Austin. When Jessie traveled, she was always on a budget and made her way there on mule if that was the least expensive method to reach her destination. She confused the Sherpa and porters because she didn't expect her campsite to resemble a hotel with food prepared by a French chef. She was there to live alongside them, hardships and all.

This Pullman was a little different from the ones her uncle hired, though. The parlor area had dark paneling and wall lamps, curtains and Axminister carpet like a four-star hotel. The furniture had soft, plum colored velvet covering heavily carved rosewood frames which consisted of a sofa with four matching chairs. A dining table with four cushioned chairs and a chandelier swinging to the movement of the train filled the rest of the room.

There was a passageway leading to the bedroom, which was also paneled and had a coffered ceiling. The large four-poster bed with thick feather mattress and bright white sheets took up most of the space. An attached bathing room had a heater for the water that was held in a separate compartment. A chair with a lid that opened to expose the train tracks speeding by beneath them finished the facilities. All the necessities of home.

Food was available from the dining car and it was the most luxurious form of travel for Jessie since she took a White Lines ship from England. They would have two days alone together with little to occupy their time – except make love. Her appetite for her husband seemed insatiable.

Jessie and Ben, both reading the newspaper, sat in the parlor portion of the Pullman Ben had hired for the trip, hoping its more comfortable ride would keep Jessie from being so sick during the day. It seemed to be working because she hadn't complained of being ill and it was almost bedtime. His male member was already anticipating their joining and he found himself humming.

"Ben," she said breathlessly. Ben looked over the top of his paper to find his wife smiling in a way he had never seen her smile before.

Unsure if he was misreading her signals answered, "Yes, dear?" He held his breath waiting for her reply.

"Are you ready for bed?" Her voice was throaty, bringing Ben's full attention on completing his mission.

"Are you asking because you are tired or because you aren't?" He smiled as her lips widened into a laugh. "Me, too. Can I help you with anything?" He did help her out of her chair and then walked with her to the bedroom where she turned into his arms.

"Do you think this is wrong somehow? That we should not be this happy?" she asked him as he bent and covered her mouth with his.

After a few moments he asked her, "Does that seem wrong? And why don't you think you deserve to be happy?"

"I'm not sure, merely a feeling that hangs over me at times. If we hadn't been captured would we be together tonight or would we have shaken hands back in Texas, said goodbye and never looked back?" He could tell she was seriously asking and watching the play of emotions on his face.

"I can't answer for you, but I had no plans of shaking your hand and then letting you walk away. I was holding back in the camp because my superior officers thought I had the maturity to do the job, of protecting you even when they thought you were a man. I wasn't going to let them down. I figured once we got back to town, you and I could have a long talk, maybe I could show you what I thought of you then." He pushed his hips into hers, letting her know how interested he was in her right that minute.

"I'm afraid I would have gotten on that stage and left like I always did. I never thought of myself as being married let alone as a mother. Now I'm practically both."

"And I didn't see myself as travelling all over the world with a fantastic wife who will be having my child by the summer. Marriage is always a give and take. Lives were made to change with those needs and right now it's important you get to do what you always wanted to do. Later, we may have to change again for the child's needs." He kissed her again. "Did you change your mind about being tired?"

"No, for some reason I really like not sleeping with you." She smiled as he began to remove his trousers as quickly as possible before helping her. Jessie pushed her pelvis into him, wrapping one leg up around his thigh while he placed his hands on her buttocks and lifted her so he could enter her without moving further.

Soon they were both out of control, breathing heavily with Jessie's searching hands urging them to higher and higher heights before reaching the peak and floating down to earth. Ben was leaning against the wall holding Jessie as she collapsed onto his chest, both trying to catch their breaths.

"Are you all right?" He panted, still holding her to him.

"Better than all right," she answered through heavy breaths.

Ben was able to move first and placed Jessie on the open bed. Laughing, he shook his head as if to clear it. "This is madness, Jessie. I'm afraid I'm going to hurt you, this thing between us is so powerful."

Jessie brushed his hair back in place from where she had wrapped her arms around him to keep him from leaving her, asking innocently, "Isn't this the way it always is?"

"Not from my experience. I can't seem to get enough of you and what I think will be a simple matter of comforting each other turns into…" He waved his hands toward the wall where he had been leaning. "Whatever that was." At her questioning expression, he tried to explain the difference. "I'm pretty average. Most of us Rangers don't have time to form any kind of relationship with a woman since we're moved around so we depend on the working girls. I would pick out a girl who seemed friendly and I did what I did, but I wasn't worried about who she had been with before me or who she would be with after me."

He became more serious. "With you I find I am sort of protective, possessive, but it's more than that. Like this morning, I didn't like the way Morgan helped you down from the buggy, made me edgy and he's my brother. Then I realized I stepped between you and a man who had glanced over at you a moment too long. He wasn't doing anything but looking, and I resented that civilization prevented me from punching him in the nose." He finished, pride and shame warring with each other.

Jessie was quiet, thinking and then confessed, "I felt the same way about the slender blond."

"What slender blond?" he asked, not understanding what she was talking about.

"The one who kept dropping things in front of you, trying to get your attention in the train station. She bent over in front of you so often I thought she was presenting." She said it with such disdain that both of them laughed at the vision.

97

"I'm sorry I missed that. I really don't believe I saw her."

"And that's why I didn't pull her false hair pieces out of her overly-elaborate style." She stroked his shoulder and chest as he lay next to her, no longer noticing the scars that had made him the man he was.

"You're the anthropologist, what do you think it means?" he asked, hoping she would come to the same conclusion he had a few days ago.

"I'm not sure. I've studied other peoples' mating habits, but it was more difficult to get true knowledge of early marriage activities. Many cultures hold with having the couple leave the rest of the village for a while, others have a ceremony or dance where everyone in the village goes off and copulates afterwards."

"Copulates? You mean they all go off into the bushes and have sex? Just one on one?" He was getting into the idea of a village orgy.

"Relax, I don't foresee us going and needing to study any of those villages again."

He felt his skin warm again as he listened to his wife, imagining her with him in those bushes, too. "Are these villages written about in your books? Do you have any of those books with you?" He reached over to stroke her bare breasts.

"Ben, we'll have to find a way to control our attraction to each other or territorial behavior or whatever this is. We'll need to be able to handle it when we are in public which will be for the next couple of weeks." She moved allowing him more access to her body.

"Do you think if we just, you know, take care of things every two or three hours we won't go overboard like we just did?" He was serious and worried his hunger for his wife wasn't going to fade anytime soon. Morgan will have a field day with this if it continued.

She shook her head wondering how long it would take for her not to be so passionate with this man. "I don't think I ever studied any culture that had coitus quiet that often, so possibly the need wears off although with me already being pregnant there isn't a natural reason to be so, so…" She had no words for her desire, passion, hunger for this man. No other man even seemed to come close, no matter how physically attractive he was. Jessie thought that was why she believed Ben when he said he didn't remember the blond that morning.

"Horny?" he teased. "The word I think you're searching for is horny or randy or aroused or…."

"I get the idea. I know the words, but not what they really meant. These feelings seem so intense between us. You have felt them before then?" she asked, the anthropologist in full force and Ben knew it.

"I didn't say that. I was simply giving you some more common terms for our feelings, but ours, mine at least, are stronger than anything I've gone through before and I thought puberty was rough. At least you're accommodating." He smiled at her and became friendlier with his hands.

"Really Ben, this conversation is getting you aroused? I suppose if I were talking about pollination between various plants you would think about our, our um-m-m, being together?" She felt exasperated by his total lack of control but proud at the same time. That she could arouse him so easily and so often now they were married. She wondered if it would have been the same if she had stayed with him after her research was complete in the desert.

"Maybe, but right now. I'm having trouble focusing on anything besides you in this bed. See?" He offered her a peek under the covers.

She knew she blushed at his blatant act of trying to get her to become as aroused as he was again and then capitulated moving closer. "Do you think we could take a little more time to really get to know each other?"

"I'll take all night if that's what you want. I'm never going to leave you." He leaned over and kissed her mouth, his hand on one breast. It didn't take all night, but they spent more time with one another, learning more about what each of them liked. In the morning, Jessie woke Ben by rubbing her body up and down his, letting him wake up to her needing him again.

CHAPTER SIX

"Jessie? You still feeling all right?" Ben asked as they huddled in the bow of the sturdy fishing boat hired to take them to the Florida shore. "Miguel said if you stand and look forward you should feel better. I'll hold you up if that helps."

"I thought I was finished with being sick. I haven't been plagued with this since we were married." Her face was pale and her skin clammy-cold even in the heat.

"I think it has to do with the water being a little rough in the bay. This isn't the same as our taking the riverboat down the Mississippi. Let me help you and see if Miguel's suggestion works for expectant mothers." Ben stood behind her, letting the breeze blow into her face. "Better?"

"I think it's working. I don't have the urge to hang over the edge of the boat again." She seemed to be trying to keep her sense of humor since this trip wasn't exactly as she planned it.

"Good, I don't know how else to get to our destination and we won't have to be on this for very long. We'll hit shore by evening and then there will be land beneath you again." He had worried the trip would be too much for her and the baby.

Jessie closed her eyes and leaned back against him. "I've always been a good ocean traveler. I was born on a ship and have traveled to China and the Sandwich Islands and Australia and never got sick no matter how

101

rough the seas. Now I can't cross Mexico Bay? It's not more than bath water in comparison."

"Maybe the baby will be a land lubber." He teased into her ear, holding his hand over her stomach in some form of protection of his child, too.

"Probably will want to travel on horseback like his father."

The thought of the baby being a real person with likes and dislikes, moods, a will of its own, hit Ben in the gut. Up till now he had imagined it always as a small bundle of sweet-smelling baby who needed to be fed and changed and protected, but it wouldn't always remain that way. Too soon it will have other wants and needs and to make its own decisions. Now Ben was clammy and felt sick to his stomach. Sometimes life became too real, too soon.

The couple remained leaning against the bulwark, both quiet with their own thoughts. Finally, Miguel, a Mexican national living in New Orleans yelled in Spanish that the shore was in sight. The couple stood straighter to stare into the horizon, barely making out the grayish bumps riding the waves. As the boat chugged closer, the grey turned to greens and the bumps took shape as trees and brush lining the coast. Ben left Jessie so he could help Miguel prepare for anchoring. They would need to go in by small rowboat because the bigger fishing boat couldn't get in close enough to unload the supplies directly due to the sandbars right off shore.

Jessie watched the men ready the skiff. Ben took her first along with a few boxes of supplies. At shore, he climbed into the surf, lifted her out and carried her to shore. "Go up towards the sea grapes where you won't get wet."

Not waiting, Jessie took a small box with her then continued to make trips carrying the lighter weight items making a pile past the sea grapes where the normal tide wouldn't reach them.

Miguel, wearing white baggy shirt and pants with a wide colorful scarf as a belt wrapped around his considerable girth, was in the last boatload and helped Ben carry the heavier items off the beach before they all stopped to rest.

Miguel said in Spanish, "When I was hunting for a good campsite, I found one further inland. You will stay dry unless there is a hurricane, but it is too early in the year so I don't think there should be a problem. Just follow the marks on the trees, see there is the first one." He pointed to a gash in the palm tree a few yards from them about four feet off the ground.

"You really got us close to the campsite when you steered your boat in here," Jessie told him.

Miguel beamed from the admiration. "I made mental pictures of the coast so I could do so. I catch the most fish because I can find the best places the fish like to go to hide from the bigger fish. I can always find them there and cast my nets. Sometimes I get both the little fish and the big fish so either way I win." He laughed.

Ben replied in Spanish, "You may have to tell me those secrets because I intend to supplement our supplies with fresh fish. Dried meat and smoked fish are not high on my list and my better half says we can't decimate the animals living here naturally or we will bring about the extinction of the whole Florida everglades."

"Que?" Miguel turned to Jessie for interpretation

Jessie, whose Spanish wasn't as good as Ben's said, "He's joshing you. I said no such thing. I simply told him it would be best if we ate what we brought rather than hunt or harm too many animals native to the shoreline."

Ben teased as he moved the crate of live chickens Jessie insisted upon bringing for fresh eggs and meat while they were there. "Which means we can't let any of these stupid chickens we brought escape or the whole ecological system will be thrown off balance and the world will tip on its axis."

As Miguel turned to Jessie again, she put up her hand. "Ben is teasing me, Miguel. Nothing he said is true." She gave a look at her husband that said, 'stop upsetting Miguel'.

"She is right, Miguel. I am only teasing her because I am the one who will probably be in charge of feeding them and making sure they don't get eaten by large snakes." Ben kept teasing Jessie. She told him recently that large spiders came first on her list of least liked things followed by snakes, not really a surprise for a female. What was a surprise was that she would admit to the fears at all.

Waving as he got into the rowboat, Miguel told them he would be back next month with the supplies on the list he already had. He wouldn't be back before then unless there was a big storm or other catastrophe. With that thought on their minds, Ben and Jessie set up camp on the edge of the beach for the night.

They debated about setting up the tent when a bevy of mosquitoes became inquisitive and the couple decided they could best protect themselves in a tent with netting covering the openings. They ate right out of the cans, not bothering to try to get a fire going in an area where everything seemed damp from the salt water spray. Halfway through the cans they exchanged them so each one got some of the beef stew and the peaches. They shared a baguette and water and then it was time for bed, the sun setting over the bay in the west.

Ben, cocooning Jessie as the night got cooler, spoke into her ear, "Are you really feeling better? I won't try to make you go back if you aren't so you can tell me the truth."

"You won't be able to make me go back for at least a month when Miguel returns. I promise if I'm still sick by then, I'll push Miguel into the bay in my rush to get to his boat. But stop worrying, Ben, I was over being ill and I'm not going to succumb to it now."

"It's been a busy day. I hope we won't need to do anything more till morning. That damn rooster better not take it into his head to crow at dawn or I'll cover him with a canvas tarp." For the first night since their marriage, they didn't make love and both were asleep within moments.

That damn rooster did start crowing at daybreak and Ben cussed it from beneath the covers tightening his arm around his wife. She liked the way she felt up against his manhood. "You still feeling all right, Jessie?" He allowed one hand to move to her breasts.

Yawning, she smiled. "Absolutely. You want to make me breakfast? You did say you wanted to be in charge of the camp, didn't you?"

"Just give me a minute and I can do that for you." He nuzzled the back of her neck and pulled the back of her gown up, bringing her body closer to him.

"A minute, huh?" Jessie teased as she leaned her head back for his kiss and began to enjoy his morning attentions as much as she always did.

105

Later, after Jessie had gathered the eggs and Ben had actually cooked them, the couple walked the path toward their final campsite, each carrying some of the supplies. They approved of the space Miguel had selected of a clearing with few over-hanging palm trees. There were smaller trees to protect them from the salt-water winds that came off the bay and enough open area to protect them and their supplies from animals and crawling insects hiding in the undergrowth surrounding them.

The couple spent most of the day moving their supplies and setting up the tent again. This time Jessie dug a trench around the tent to carry the rainwater away from their living space. Ben set up a kitchen area using some of the wooden crates then stored the invaluable fresh water where it would be the safest. The privy was the last and Ben made it so they could move it when they needed to along with the canvass curtains for privacy.

Later he moved the chickens away from the main living area and promised Jessie he would build some legs for their crates to keep snakes and other predators away from them. The line for drying clothes was hung between two of the sturdy palms and he looked worriedly up at the green coconuts hanging like clusters of grapes above them.

"I was looking at those, too. I've been in areas with coconuts before. They cut them down or they can drop on your head and kill you."

"How did they get them down before they fell on their heads?" He stared up at the otherwise un-scary fruit.

"The young men would simply climb the tree trunk barefoot with a machete between their teeth and cut them down with one whack." She imitated the movement. "The others had a long pole they used to knock them down, but I think they have to be riper and more dangerous to people below by that time."

"How exactly did the men do it by climbing the trunk?" Evidently, he felt ready to learn a new skill.

Jessie thought about it a minute. "They used a leather strap around the tree to hang on and went up the tree pressing their feet against the trunk and taking their weight on the strap. A strip of canvas might be strong enough to hold you. Wear gloves to protect your hands. What do you think?"

"I'll work on it a while and then see what I come up with. I only need to climb these two trees over-hanging the camp. The rest we will have to be wary of for falling coconuts."

By evening most of the gear was stashed and the food stores placed in a safe manner. The chickens' cage had been raised for protection and both Jessie and Ben were too tired to bother with cooking so they opened two more cans, sharing as they had the night before.

Once more they found themselves in the tent. This time the mattress was on a frame raised off the ground to keep them up from the plentiful number of snakes, scorpions and other crawling critters that abounded in the swamps less than a mile away. Ben said he felt like he was right back home in Texas and fell asleep soon after hearing Jessie's light breathing next to him.

The rooster woke Ben and Ben woke Jessie, and that seemed to become the morning ritual, with Jessie needing an afternoon rest, which Ben sometimes joined her for. It was a rather idyllic life. Both of them getting tan as they did their own studying and mapping during the day, wearing fewer clothes than civilization required.

There were a few cool days and rain for several days in a row, but not as cold as Texas which was right on the opposite side of the bay. The plants were more interesting to Ben and Jessie explained she was going to do the grids and leave the strings in place and return to each grid to watch the plants as they changed during their growing seasons. She explained there was less of a noticeable change in seasons in Florida and many more types of plants with edible parts than the desert presented.

Miguel made the first of six visits to the shoreline, firing a gun into the air from the boat to get Ben's attention.

Rushing to the beach, Ben prepared to help with the supplies piled on the boat's narrow deck. Jessie followed after pulling a dress on over her enlarging stomach.

"How is everyone? Does your wife still get sick?" the rotund man called out as he hit the sandbar. He brought newspapers in English, too, which was a special request made by Ben for Jessie. Miguel's wife sent freshly made Mexican dishes, knowing the limited menu of canned food would get boring after weeks of nothing else to eat. The most notable gift was the lemon drops because, Miguel, the father of several children was sure Jessie would appreciate them as much as his wife had when she had been carrying their children.

Miguel was able to stay and talk for over an hour and then promised to return in a month with more supplies. He took the letters to be posted and rowed back to the fishing boat.

The couple stood on the shore waving until the boat was out of sight and then looked at each other. Scratching his beard, which he had let grow rather than shave with salt water, Ben knew his hair was getting longer than normal for a military man and thought about having Jessie cut it someday soon. He thought about the open collar shirt with the sleeves rolled up and his trousers rolled up to the knees as well. How changed he was from the man Miguel dropped off only four weeks earlier.

Today Jessie wore a dress, but some days she dressed much as he was. Simply a shirt and rolled up trousers. Stockings and union suits were packed away till they were needed for the trip north to New Orleans, back-tracking up the Mississippi to St. Louis where Jessie would turn in her notebooks and drawings in the spring.

The weeks passed quickly, more visits by Miguel and on this last time he was accompanied by one of his sons and his wife who appeared much younger than her husband. They came on shore, bringing several loaves of bread as gifts. Miguel was very loquacious about the size of Jessie's stomach, even touching the mound with gentle hands and teasing that maybe she was having twins as his wife Margarita had once done.

Jessie insisted it was only one, but that exchange got Ben thinking after the fishing boat left to return to the mouth of the Mississippi. In bed for the night, his palm lay on the mound that had been the topic of conversation earlier when his hand was kicked right off her stomach.

"What the…. Was that the baby? Can it kick that hard already?" he asked, reality setting in about the real little stranger who would soon become part of their lives.

"It's kicked you before, whenever you squash it." She chuckled, but didn't move from where she lay. "It needs more room now, of course, but it feels things touch it from the outside and sometimes reacts. When I lay out on the beach to dry in the sun after bathing, it has a great time rolling and kicking at my hand when I place it on my stomach. I think it can actually see my hand now. It always seems to hit the mark."

Ben went back to the first part. "Do I really squash it? You mean when we make love?"

"Not really, it just moves around and gets settled somewhere else. It doesn't like me on my back any more either. Must be bony or something." She settled into a new position to keep the baby from kicking her bladder she explained.

"I hadn't noticed or didn't realize what it was. We'll have to stop until it is born." He placed his hand gently on her abdomen, waiting for the baby to kick him again.

"No, we won't have to stop until it's born. The baby is fine and will learn to move to be comfortable just as I do. We both have to share my body and you can share it sometimes, too. I have several more weeks before we'll need to find some other way to comfort you." She patted his hand on her stomach and finished, "Go to sleep, Ben, the baby has already quieted for the night."

Ben thought about the baby for another hour before finally patting the mounded belly and whispering, "I'll never leave you, either."

Their morning lovemaking was a little strained until Ben took the offered alternative of curling up around Jessie and bringing her satisfaction as he had when they first slept together in the tent as husband and wife. "This won't bother the baby will it?" he asked anxiously, still worried about squashing the infant.

"This will be fine, no complaint so far." He kissed her neck and cheek, holding her breast with one hand and her stomach with the other. They finished with complete satisfaction and he whispered, "I'll feel better about it if we can make love like this for now."

"That's fine Ben, the baby really merely wants to play with you, but it seems more comfortable for me, too," she told him. "I'm realizing how much larger I've gotten in the last couple of weeks."

After all, he thought, there was only going to be one more supply drop off and then they would be leaving Florida. Time had stopped having meaning as he realized they hadn't seen another person other than Miguel and his family since landing on the sandy beach.

That brought all the worries of how Jessie was going to accept her motherhood and the limits it would place upon her. If she did allow it to place restrictions upon her. If she refused to listen to reason then he would care for the child himself. He would move back with his parents and allow them to help until he had himself established in Austin. Hoping it wouldn't come to that, he touched his wife's arm again making sure she still slept beside him. As if she had already decided to leave him. As if she had already left to do the profession she loved and felt she could only do in other far-off places.

If he gave her that option, or more like, allowed her to choose that path would she also choose to stay married and make his home her home at some time in the future? He couldn't see himself with anyone else. Couldn't want a different wife or mother for his children. He prayed this child would unit them and not drive them apart. That their vows to one another would make a bond neither would be willing to break.

Ben was off exploring the shoreline, charting it and following any rivers and tributaries inland leaving Jessie to her work. He had become very adept at dodging the alligators and had forbidden her from trying to draw or study them in any way. She was supposed to be studying plants only and any animal or insects were secondary and for her own education.

The chickens' eggs had become a target for several types of small rodents and snakes so finding one winding its way up the wooden leg supporting the chicken crate off the ground wasn't that surprising. Ben was inland so Jessie took her hand gun and shot the head off, leaving the body writhing on the ground. It wasn't a snake she was familiar with so she decided to gather the pieces and make a drawing of the yellow and black banded reptile to study when she got back to a library.

The squawking of the notably upset chickens was a distraction. Bending to pick up the decapitated head, she felt a prick on her finger and noticed a drop of venom still on the other protruding fang. Jessie immediately poured water over the wound and ran toward the shoreline to scrub the finger in the salt water, using sand to get any residue off her skin.

Within half an hour she was nauseous, her arms were shaking and she felt she was running a fever. She knew it would be dangerous for her baby if her fever got too high so she laid down at the edge of the ocean with more than half her body submerged. Jessie wasn't sure how long she had been in the water or when she began losing consciousness, unable to form coherent thoughts, her mouth and eyes dry.

Was this to be how Ben found her when he returned? Dead of a poisonous viper's bite because she was too stubborn, too wrapped up in her own wants to take care of herself for her child's sake? If she lost this baby due to her own hubris at wanting to prove to everyone at university she was as good as a man, she would never forgive herself. She should die, as well, for not being the mother her own mother was.

Her mother had been as tenacious in learning about other cultures and still found a way to care for Jessie. Jessie fought for consciousness as she felt the life in her ebb and flow with the tide now beginning to go out.

Coming back along the shore from a long day out, Ben squinted to make out the shape laying at the shoreline. He ran to Jessie's side as soon as he realized what it was he saw. He dragged her onto the beach of sand and broken shells calling her name.

"Jessie, Jessie, wake up, honey. Tell me what happened, where are you hurt?" He stroked his hands over her body, finding the small scrapped finger and dismissing it as being of no importance, continuing to try to find a more serious wound.

He finally decided a spider or snake must be the culprit and the small place of broken skin became a focus for him. Ben knew the injury was too old to cut or suck out the poison, which was what he would have done right after a snakebite in Texas. Now he was at a loss as to what to do.

Carrying Jessie past the sea grapes, he laid her down as she became conscious, showing signs of delirium from the poison running through her body. She was trembling, but not just from the cold of the gulf's water. All Ben could do was hold her body close to his and pray the venom wasn't strong enough to take her from him. He didn't want to think what it may be doing to the baby.

Holding her in his arms, Ben rocked her repeating begging quietly. "Don't leave me."

As the sun began to warm the beach, Jessie woke slowly. "Ben is the baby all right?" Placing her hands on her stomach as if trying to protect their child.

Ben wasn't sure how to answer her, but tried to keep her calm. "I think its fine. I was afraid for you when I found you half in the surf. Everything else seems just as it was. Did you get bitten? Did you see what it was?"

She struggled to sit up and leaned against him breathing shallowly. "Not bitten exactly, but I got enough snake venom to make me sick. It's not something I would want to repeat that's for sure. I was running a fever and afraid for the baby. I had to cool myself down, keep the baby cooler and the ocean seemed the logical choice. I still feel oddly."

"Let's get you back to camp and out of this wet dress. I don't think you have a fever now. In fact, you feel too cold to me." He pulled the dress off her as she stood, then carried her naked to the camp.

He insisted she rest for the day and after disposing carefully of the beheaded snake, stayed in camp taking care of her needs. This incident brought home to both of them how seriously dangerous it was with only the two of them against a tropical forest and swamp full of unknown killers.

Although he kept busy, his mind on other matters. Like how to protect his wife and child out here in the wilderness. Rough living was fine for him. He was used to it, strong enough to fight off an attacker, use weapons with brute force. But Jessie wasn't very big or strong in that way.

It wasn't only that she was a woman - she was his woman. He wanted her to be free to do the work she felt suited her, but she had his child inside her and that had to count for something. He couldn't agree for her to take the baby when she went to Alaska. There may not be poisonous snakes and alligators, but there were bears and wolves. Both known to attack vulnerable victims.

Looking over at her resting, he didn't want to have this conversation now. She was still ill from the snake venom and they didn't know how the baby would be affected. He knew she didn't mean to get bitten, but the outcome was the same. He could have lost her. Lost both of them. There were many good things in society and she had to agree with him because once he had her home in Texas, he wasn't going to let her leave alone.

Jessie had plenty of time to worry about the dangers of her chosen life style to her child, how having a child was going to impede her knowledge and ability to focus on her career. She didn't like the conclusions she was coming to.

How her parents had done so was coming back to her. They had both taught her and cared for her in turns, but it could not be said she had a normal up-bringing. She rarely had children her own age to play with. Her parents hadn't wanted to alter the lives of the indigenous peoples they were studying by introducing Jessie and her play activities. They feared such activities could alter the natural evolution of the native children's lives. Instead, she was kept separated and limited with such toys other children knew. Most of her time was spent in watching her parents study and being read to from books written for university students. A child growing up alone in a world of adults.

How was she going to travel and study unknown civilizations and still not affect her child's own future growth and knowledge? She couldn't find a satisfying answer to her worries. These same worries plagued her during the quiet moments just before sleep for the weeks she had left in Florida.

Today's fear could have lasting effects on her child. Her heart raced at any sort of twinge or pain fearing she had brought on her labor or her body was rejecting the fetus. She breathed easier when she felt the usual kicks and pokes that came every evening, as if knowing she was thinking about the little being inside her.

She rubbed her stomach, but this time the baby didn't kick her hand or make any contact with the outside world. "I'm sorry, little one. I really need to take more care of you. I'll be better I promise."

Finally, the trip home was happening. Ben had been anxious about it ever since Jessie's reaction to the snake venom. The memory of her illness making Ben break out in a cold sweat. The closer they got to the port of New Orleans and medical care, the more he would be able to look on the trip as something good for Jessie. The final study of her career as she retired and raised their family. That is what he hoped she would choose to do. He promised himself he would always stay close to home so he could be with his family, with Jessie, every night and would be a help-mate in all things.

Ben had been up front of the fishing boat with Miguel while Jessie rested after complaining of a headache, which was unusual for her. He glanced back to see her bent over the boat's side, losing her breakfast to the fish.

"Still don't have your sea legs, Honey?" Teasing as he came up behind her to help her back to the soft pile of canvas and blankets, he had made for her to rest on.

He turned her in his arms then realized her eyes were shiny with fever and his mind raced back to the day he had found her submerged in the surf, her life seemingly hanging by a thread. "Jessie, have you been bitten? Do you know what's wrong?" Frantically he began searching her body for signs of another venomous bite.

"N-n-no," she said through shattering teeth. "I've h-h-had th-this bef-f-fore. It's m-m-malaria. I-I-I th-thought I-I-I was immune n-n-now."

"Do we have any medicine for this? I remember you telling me you brought something for me, in case I came down with it." He hoped she could tell him which concoction it was in the well-stocked medical kit.

"Q-q-quinine. W-W-Warb-burg's Tincture." She forced the words out, trying to keep from shivering too much to be understood.

"I'll be right back. Here, cover up. I have to find the right pile of boxes." He went over the rolling deck to their belongings packed up from the campsite, trying to remember which crate held the precious medical supplies.

He brought back a colored bottle with a smoky liquid inside and asked frustrated, "How much do I give you? The bottle doesn't say anything."

Jessie took the uncorked bottle and put it to her lips, drinking a little of the liquid then handing it back to him. "I'll b-b-be all right in a little while. I need to r-r-rest."

Ben sat down with Jessie in his lap, his mind a whirl with worry for his wife and infant. How was he going to keep them safe if Jessie insisted she should be able to keep going into these God forsaken areas to compile a list of plants or insects or animals. It didn't matter, nothing was as important as her safety and the safety of their child. But how did he convince his wife without her leaving him behind? She had her own money and she had enough courage. What would it take to put aside her career for him if she wouldn't for her own child?

Jessie rested fitfully and by the time the boat landed in port, Ben had decided to change their plans.

"Miguel, send all these books and drawings on to St. Louis as you did with the others, she sent with you before. They will know what to do with them. I'm taking Jessie straight to my father's ranch where my mother can look after her before the baby comes."

Miguel agreed it would probably be the best for her. Ben also purchased more of the tincture which was readily available around the swampy area of New Orleans.

Waking, Jessie didn't seem to have strength to converse or complain of the change in plans. Ben made arrangements to take the Texas-New Orleans Railroad to Houston where one of his father's men would meet them and drive them out to the ranch unless Ben thought Jessie should see a doctor first. He wasn't going to worry about what his wife would think of his plans. She was his responsibility and he would answer any complaints after she was stronger.

CHAPTER SEVEN

The doctor in Houston, an older man with grey liberally infused in his hair and mustache, told him, "I don't know much about the type of malaria your wife has, Mr. Edwards. Each area has its own strain and since she told you she's had it before, she probably had some immunity built up which bodes well for her and the baby."

Ben was relieved until the doctor continued, "In the early months of pregnancy it can cause a miscarriage. Your wife is sufficiently along so that the baby seems safe enough but malaria is known to bring on an early birth, too. She's not due for another eight weeks, you say? Pretty sure on that are you?"

"Very sure. The twelfth of September." He stated it with such surety the doctor didn't question how Ben knew so exactly.

"Then I don't see why she shouldn't travel by wagon and when you get home have the doctor there check her over again. Never can be too careful with these things." He stood, making the small examination room seem even smaller with the three of them occupying it.

Jessie had been too tired to add or argue with what Ben was doing, merely following as he instructed. Ben hoped she wouldn't be too angry when she got strong enough, but he did what he felt he had to do to protect her and their child. Keeping true to his promise to protect them and never leave her.

His father's ranch hand was waiting outside the doctor's office in the buckboard on a busy street of the city. As soon as Jessie was cocooned in a pile of blankets on a thick straw mattress, they were on a road out of town. Ben didn't want to talk much, trying to think about what was to come when he finally got back to the ranch. He knew he and Jessie would be welcomed. His mother had practically adopted Jessie on the spot in Washington and thrown him out with the bath water. And that was before she learned Jessie was carrying her grandchild. The problem was whether Jessie would stay in one spot for the nearly two months before the baby was born or whether there was going to be an argument as to Ben's amount of control over her.

Ben soon learned. Jessie, finally feeling better and more rested, was silently smoldering over what she thought as Ben's needless change of their plans. Of her going to St. Louis while she finished up the study along with renting a house there until after the baby's birth. He wasn't sure she would remain as he hoped she would.

When they arrived at the Edwards' property as the sun was setting, Jessie got the impression of a large two-story ranch with a wraparound porch. The large windows were warmed by the lamps inside and a massive stone fireplace that took up one wall. The living area had several large leather chairs and a sofa with a Navajo blanket over the back. The room was homey and warm and inviting with woven rugs on the polished wood floor and brightly striped curtains lining each of the windows. But Jessie didn't feel at home.

Ben's parents were as warm and welcoming as the home, but again, not what Jessie was used to. The Major, still using his rank since more than half the ranch hands were ex-rangers who had served under him, was pleasant. He was slim and tall and had a mustache only with more gray than brown in it. Ben certainly would remain handsome if his father was anything to go by. She liked him and the way he showed his feeling toward his wife even now so many years after marrying her. She liked it but feared it, also. It showed loyalty was part of the family traits and that worried her about the time when she would leave here to become her own woman once again.

Ben's mother was all excited and then all worried as she learned of the dangers Jessie and the baby had been through. Emily, couldn't have been more considerate or a better mother-in-law. She evidently didn't expect Jessie to do anything besides sleep, eat and grow her grandchild. Jessie no longer feared Morgan, but the shadow of the tipi he slept in outside the ranch house sent shivers down her spine. A reminder of a time in her life too gruesome to think about.

She waited till they were in their room before telling Ben exactly what she thought of being brought back to Texas, back to Comanche territory, "Ben, we discussed this and I thought you understood my feelings."

"Honey, I know what you said, but that was before the snake bite and the malaria. The doctor said it could bring on an early birth." He seemed to try to make her understand the danger she was in while also taking charge.

"There are doctors and hospitals in St. Louis. We should have continued on there as I had planned." She emphasized the last three words.

"That would have taken longer, either by train or riverboat. I thought having a woman around you would be a help. My mother can help you through this better than I can," Ben explained, trying to reason with her.

"Then I suggest we let her. Find another room to sleep in. I'll be fine here by myself. I'll ask your mother for anything else I might need," she snapped back at him angrily.

Knowing she was tired and still ill, Ben took his bag into one of the other empty bedrooms, hoping his wife would be in a better mood in the morning. She wasn't. She came down for the midday meal and then went back to her room. Resting, it seemed, but no one knew for certain.

Ben's mother soothed him. "New mothers-to-be often need time to be alone. After all, you have just spent more than six months together. Jessie needs to prepare herself for being a mother and for some women that means making plans."

He understood that part of things. Jessie, although able to think quickly when the need arose, liked to make long-range plans and then stick to them. He knew that was the main reason she was angry with him, for altering the plans, even though he felt he had adequate reason for doing so.

Ben tried to talk with Jessie about the baby and the future. He was trying to decide whether to stay living at the ranch or build another place for his family on the property a little way away from the main compound. Every time he brought it up, they got off topic and Jessie went to rest in her room leaving Ben with mixed thoughts. One day Jessie seemed ready to discuss their future, but it wasn't what Ben thought she would say.

"I've thought a lot about these last few months and although I enjoyed our time together, I realized we are not like my parents. We will never be a couple who works together on projects because we're not interested in the same things. I feel we should separate as soon as the baby is born. I'll set up a home in one of the larger cities and hire a nursemaid. You may visit as often as you like. I will accept work that takes me away no longer than a year at a time. If the child is a boy, he can visit you for a few weeks during term breaks, anywhere you want him to be with you until he's old enough to decide for himself."

Incensed at her high-handed planning of his child's life he asked, "But not if it's a girl?"

"What do you know about girls? You would have nothing to talk about with a girl. I think a boy needs a father figure to look up to, to learn how to be a man. All the cultures have some sort of rite or ritual, but here he would have to get his cues from an adult male." She was reasonable and rational, having thought the whole thing out, planned their life.

"A daughter needs a father figure, also, especially in this culture where her cues are gotten from how her father and mother interact with each other," he said without hesitation, proving to Jessie their conversations about cultures hadn't been a complete waste of her time.

"I see you've been paying attention to my books, but it is of no matter. I will make sure my daughter is well acclimatized with her culture." She walked to the window and stared out.

"I will want time with the child regardless of the sex. I will not abandon my child." Ben followed her to the window over-looking the tipi, which was always present at the side of the house in case Morgan returned for a visit. His brother never slept in the ranch house when he

123

was here. "I'm beginning to realize how strong you feel about leaving me, about your plans for your future without me. Jessie, why don't you do as your parents did? Study those cultures in the safety of a more modern society like your parents raised you in. Save the more dangerous areas for when the child is older and can be sent to school. We can be together then and I'll take care of the children and you…."

"Ben, there will be no other children." She shook her head slowly. "Not between you and me. I will give you a divorce. Once I leave here the clock starts ticking and it will be a few short years before you can file under abandonment. You're still young enough to marry again and have a real family with a home or ranch. That isn't a life for me. I never meant to lead you on, but those safe areas you said I was raised in are true. But that was twenty years ago. Now the only new, unstudied cultures are farther afield in South America, the Pacific Islands or the Far East. No one knows how many are left, but all of them are incredibly far and incredibly dangerous. Not a place to bring a child or husband."

Losing hope, he asked, "So you couldn't see yourself as having a home base here, in Texas, living with me between your trips?"

Jessie was tired of arguing for her right to the life she had planned. "I hate being here knowing that tipi is right outside waiting for Morgan. What if he brings someone back with him? More Comanche? I don't feel comfortable here. I know everyone has been more than accommodating to my whims and less than polite actions. I didn't ask to come here and I may yet decide to go north before this baby is born. I can let you know where I can be found after the birth." She was telling him honestly, almost desperately that she needed to be away from him and from the place where her life had changed so dramatically such a short time ago.

"No, please stay. I will leave. I can take on an offered assignment for surveying and purchasing land for the railroad and you can rest here until the baby. Don't make any more plans. I understand you don't want me part of them. That you'll move on as soon as the baby is born."

Jessie felt terrible because she saw tears in this strong man's eyes and she was the cause. And she hated them both for it.

Ben left the next day and although Emily, Ben's mother, didn't say anything she wasn't happy that Ben had left. Emily, it seemed, was bent on being the best mother-in-law and future grandmother. While bringing out the knitting patterns for baby items, she assured Jessie the baby would need, they began to make their selections. Jessie wasn't sure any living thing needed quiet so many clothes but didn't argue. Merely accepting the proffered yarn and needles and knit as she was instructed.

She and Emily spent most of their days getting ready for the baby, speaking of nothing more personal than the weather and the garden Emily was planning to put in now spring was here. Jessie was rocking in one of the chairs on the wide porch, not really paying any attention to the world as another day passed by when a strange feeling went through her body, not a pain exactly but something. She stood to ask Emily if it could have anything to do with the baby when she felt water run down her stockings and petticoat. Before she could call out, Emily was coming towards her with a cup of tea in her hand.

"What is it, Jessie, you're looking strange." She put out her empty hand to help Jessie sit back down.

"I think my water broke. I think I'm having the baby, but there isn't any pain," she said in wonderment.

"That can happen, but sit back down. It sounds like the birth is a long way off. We may as well sit here in the sun as anywhere else. I'll check on things in the house to make sure we're ready for this and bring you something else to put on."

When Emily returned, Jessie was squeezing the arms of the chair and trying to catch her breath. The older woman said, "Maybe I was wrong. First babies usually take their time, but you seem to be further along already. I'm going to send for Ben and the doctor."

"No, not yet. I don't think it's that close. I've been to many births in the cultures I studied and the pains were much closer together and appeared to be more severe." Jessie accepted help to get into the dry nightdress with long sleeves Emily had brought out.

The pains seemed to have gone as quickly as they had arrived and Jessie was glad she hadn't allowed anyone to be sent for the doctor or Ben. She would have felt so foolish having everyone waiting on her when this would have been a false start.

"I wish I would have sent one of the men for Ben, Jessie, it doesn't seem right to leave him out."

"If I would have had it in hospital, he wouldn't be a participant. It's better he doesn't have this endless waiting. It's not as if he could help, although some cultures have the father cut the umbilical cord." Jessie was talking to keep her own mind off the pain that was beginning to grow and wash over her body like a high surf.

Bending forward, the discomfort left her body allowing Jessie some respite. Where had they come from so quickly? She was worried the doctor wouldn't arrive in time, although she and Jessie had talked of the older woman being experienced with helping other women give birth.

Emily left and returned wearing the buckskins she had on when Major Edwards had rescued her. She had shown them to Jessie when they found them in the sewing room looking for blanket material. They seemed to fit the older woman and Jessie could picture her mother-in-law working the tipi skins or cooking over an open fire. The loose deerskin dress fringed at the sleeves and hemline, leggings and moccasins all reminded Jessie of that day less than nine months ago. The only thing familiar was Emily's hair style which was left up in the favored twist.

She approached Jessie. "Come, it is time for us to go to the tipi."

"What do you mean? Aren't I having the baby upstairs in my bedroom?" Jessie asked unsure she wanted to give birth in a tipi, the same sort of place this child was conceived.

"It is the only way I know, Jessie. I had Morgan surrounded by the chief's woman folk who I thought would make things harder for me, but they thought giving birth was painful enough and didn't add to the pain. The second, Ben's father was my only help, but his being there in the tipi made it easier. That's why I sent for Ben as well as the doctor, but I don't think this baby is going to wait for either of them."

Trying not to moan through the next pain, Jessie finally spoke. "All the birth's I've attended have been in about the same sort of area as a tipi so I'll live through it too. This was one time I thought I was going to be modern and give birth in the hospital under sedation of chloroform. Instead I find myself at the very basic of human experiences." Jessie stopped walking as another contraction took over her body, stronger than any of the others, a strong pressure between her legs making her want to squat.

The tipi had been cleared of the buffalo robes and blankets, in their stead was a colorful rug. A hole lined with leather and filled with water seemed out of place in the otherwise smooth ground.

"I was just finishing up. The rocks have been heating in the fire pit outside and I will get those next. Lay down on the rug with your head between those two stakes. They will give you something to hold on to when the pain gets worse," Emily explained as she dug a second hole next to the first.

"It's going to get worse than this?" Jessie waited a moment for the contraction to pass before moving to do as Emily told her.

"I'll get the rocks. There is still some time," Emily told Jessie as she lifted the tipi flap, leaving Jessie in the tipi redolent of buffalo hide and buckskin. The scents mingling with the pain and fear made Jessie remember another tipi and another time. She wondered if Emily did, too.

Emily returned carrying several round rocks in a leather sling and dumped them sizzling into the water as the heat was transferred from the hot rocks to the cooler water. She went out for more until the sizzling lessened as the water became as hot as the rocks she had been placing into it.

"We'll let that cool. It's to be used to clean the infant and you after the birth."

Jessie's body was gripped by a much stronger contraction. She grabbed onto the stakes grimacing until the pain finally eased.

"I wish there was something more I could do for you," her mother-in-law said.

Jessie talked mostly to keep her mind off waiting for the next pain. "Some cultures have herbs and elixirs they use, but nothing has been found to work except chloroform. Then there is a danger of death if the mother is given too much. There are several more common plants used to abort a child or to bring on labor." Before she could stop herself, she asked, "Did you ever think of that?"

Emily didn't pretend not to hear or understand. "No, I loved Morgan from the moment I realized I was with child. I worried more that the squaws would harm him because he was half white, but that isn't their way. Children are welcomed, rarely punished and then not severely. Always treated as gifts from the gods and should be cherished. They are really the only things the Comanche doesn't hold in contempt. Their children are their pride and future, but the same does not cross into children of other races. Depends on who in the tribe adopts them as to how well they are treated."

"I'm sorry I brought it up. I was merely thinking, trying to keep my mind occupied."

"That was many years ago, many years of good memories between so speaking of those times does not hurt like it did at first. It is part of my life, my past and I accept it as such. I focus on the life I've had with the Major and with my sons. Now with my grandchild."

129

Jessie didn't want to cause this kind lady any more heartache, not yet, not until she would take this child and move to the north, miles from Texas and the Comanche Nation.

She wasn't sure how many hours had passed, the pains closer together and then easing and fading away to give her some relief. Jessie was flat on her back and let the need to raise her knees and place her feet on the ground guide her actions, letting the gown's hem slide down her legs to her waist as she was swept away with the need to press down and grit her teeth, holding on to the stakes for support.

"Jessie, I see the child, I see the head, but I think it is facing the wrong way. It is facing up and it should be down," Emily explained as she knelt next to her.

"What does that mean for the baby? Will it hurt it, is it dangerous?" Jessie gasped out before another contraction took hold of her body and she cried out with the pain, trying to hold back but unable to any longer.

"I'm not sure. I've never attended one before, but it can't be good. I know if the child is breach Comanche will cut it out of the mother rather than lose the child, but this isn't the same." Emily seemed to be searching to find something to calm Jessie's worries.

"Mother, I'm coming in." At first Jessie was glad Ben had made it back when she realized the voice wasn't horse enough. It was Morgan and before she could tell him to stay out, he was beside her kneeling by her head.

"We couldn't find Ben so I came back to help." At his mother's worried expression, he asked, "What's wrong? Jessie?" Then said flatly, "It's the baby. What's wrong, mother?"

"The baby is facing the wrong way up. It's dangerous and has extended the labor. I'm afraid Jessie's getting too tired. We should have made arrangements for her to be in a hospital as she wanted. They could have cut it out properly, maybe saved the baby."

"Don't let my baby die." She clutched at Morgan's bare arm, realizing he was dressed as the Comanche who had taken her hostage, his single braid entwined with one feather. The rest of his long black hair hanging loose. A long string of colored shells hung from each ear. "Save the baby, let me die. Ben will care for the baby." She heard the desperation in her own voice.

Morgan looked at the young woman, realizing his mother was right, Jessie was becoming very tired, weaker and more exhausted as he watched her since coming into the tipi. "Is there a way for you to turn the infant while still in the womb? Are your hands small enough, Mother?"

"I can try. It will need to be after a contraction, I'll have to push it back and then turn it before another contraction comes. There isn't much time between them. It may be quite painful." His mother looked at him apprehensively, trying not to see how the words would affect Jessie.

"I can do it, Emily. I can take the pain, just do it. Save my baby." He watched as Jessie prepared herself for more pain. He knew this woman had more grit than many gave her credit for.

"Alright, Little Sister, let's do this before you get too tired. We'll save you both." He gave his mother a nod once he was in place sitting behind Jessie, wrapping his

131

tattooed arms around her midriff with his bare tattooed legs along each side of her.

As soon as a contraction had passed, Emily slid her hand in and pushed the baby back and then tried turning it, but had to stop, removing her hands as another contraction nearly bent Jessie in two. He held her back against his chest, murmuring encouragement into her ear, telling her how proud Ben would be of her and although he knew she heard him she couldn't respond.

"Once more, Jessie. This time I will get it turned I promise." His mother's face still showed worry.

"Hold on, Little Sister, I'll help you," Morgan whispered in her ear. After the contraction passed, Emily put both hands into the still dilated womb and with a hand on each side of the infant gently rolled it over.

He saw that the pain was swift and took more than Jessie's breath. She sagged in exhaustion as she struggled from the darkness beckoning her.

A moment later there was a happy cry. "The head is emerging, oh, the head is almost out." An excited Emily was enraptured with the birth.

Morgan pressed downwards on Jessie's stomach, helping the contractions push the baby through the tight canal. It worked. He could tell Jessie felt relief from the pain immediately and they heard the shuddering little cry of the child, a sound between anger and fear.

"It's a boy, Little Sister, you and Ben have a son. I am happy for you both, you are blessed." He remained where he was waiting for his mother to place the baby in his arms so he could show Jessie, but Jessie had accepted the invitation from Morpheus and was sound asleep. Morgan accepted the wrapped infant while Emily buried the afterbirth in the once empty hole.

He watched as his mother took the umbilical cord to hang in a hackberry tree. If it stayed undisturbed before it rotted, the child would live a long and prosperous life. A long-held superstition of the Comanche she evidently still believed. Morgan couldn't find a reason to forbid it and allowed the custom to be performed.

Waking, Jessie found herself on a pile of buffalo skins, trying to force herself to open her eyes, knowing there was some reason it was important to open her eyes. Dragging herself into consciousness, she heard a cry from somewhere far off. No, not far off, it was a baby crying and it was getting tired, it needed help. She had to wake up and help that infant.

Forcing herself to become aware of her surroundings, she saw Ben, laying a few feet away trying to quiet his son.

"He's hungry, Jessie. I don't have anything for him, yet." He hesitated then asked, "Will you feed him?"

Jessie's stomach sank realizing Ben thought she didn't care enough for her own child to want to feed him when he was hungry. "Give him to me. I'll figure out how this all works. I've seen it done enough times." She raised her arms toward her child.

Appearing relieved, Ben brought his son to her and placed the small bundle in her arms. "I put a dry diaper on him, but that's as much as I know about an infant. There's not many books on it, either."

Jessie grimaced as her son took her nipple with a force that hurt and began to suckle. Strong pulls until she heard him swallow and quieted as he received nourishment from her body. "It really is amazing, isn't it?" she said as she watched her son. "How each thing works so well together. How each of our parts are made to work with each other part, working towards making another little being that looks just like us?" Seeing her son's hand open and close, she placed her finger in it. The infant immediately latched onto it with a strength that surprised her.

"I'm sorry I wasn't here in time. Morgan chewed me out and then praised you and said I wasn't worthy of you or this son," Ben admitted as he gazed into her eyes, searching for her feelings in the matter.

"You're a good man, Ben. I never meant to make you feel otherwise, but why would you think I wouldn't feed our son? When did I ever give you the idea I wanted to abandon this child as soon as it was born? I find that hurtful."

"It wasn't exactly what you said. I thought there would be less resentment if I took over the care of the child as soon as it was born, but he's a few weeks early. I'm not prepared. I probably shouldn't have left you, but I thought it was for the best, too. Get out of your sight before you ran from here, from me." He reached over to stroke a finger against his son's cheek making him startle and start to suckle again.

"I'm sorry, I didn't mean to wake him," he said, smiling at this turn of events.

"It's a normal reflex. He'll open his mouth when anything touches his cheeks and begin sucking," she explained to her husband. She watched him take joy in so simple a thing as watching his son nurse.

"How long will you wait till you leave me, us?" he asked. "I'll take care of him while you're away on your assignment. You can have him back until you leave again, but I think it only fair I get to care for him, watch him grow, teach him to be a man while you're away. I'm better than any nursemaid for him."

"I've made you worry about losing your child and I'm sorry for that. I was being very selfish. Please rest assured I will not separate you. I couldn't make a plan I liked because I didn't want to leave my child any more than you did. I worried about taking the child into dangerous areas where there were diseases and unknown hazards with no medical care. I was blaming you for all of it, but being in this tipi and remembering how I felt on that day, how I begged you to take me...." She was too overwhelmed to continue with that thought. "Then you promised never to leave me and I took great relief in your words. After all that, I threw it back in your face as if it were your fault."

"I feel to blame. I can't want it differently though. Look what we have because of that day." He gazed at her rather than his now sleeping son. "Would you have done it differently knowing everything you know now?"

"No, I don't think I would. I think I would have said the same thing yesterday. What's the sense of studying these other cultures if we never learn from them? Never live the culture we were born into? These other places are interesting to visit, but that only makes it more satisfying when I return to my own world. I have a life to live with you if you still want me."

He leaned over to kiss her lips. "Always. I'll never leave you."

"And I'll always be with you. I'm so sorry I tried to drive you away." She accepted more kisses.

He pulled away with a grimace. "I am supposed to be taking care of you and your needs. Are you hungry or thirsty?"

"I need you to hold me and our child. I find I am very tired again. I think I will be able to sleep peacefully now you're back with me."

"Right here? On the buffalo hides?"

"Right here with your arms around me." She agreed and closed her eyes as she felt Ben lay down behind her, feeling his arm lay across her much smaller stomach.

CHAPTER EIGHT

Jessie came into the ranch kitchen with the bright yellow curtains. "There, clean diaper and all fed. William should be quiet for a while now." She placed her son, less than four weeks old, in a cradle that seemed to float from room to room, where ever the family wanted it.

The quiet young woman called Mary, sitting at the table with a half cup of tea in front of her, smiled shyly. "He's a beautiful baby, Mrs. Edwards. Your husband must be so proud."

Jessie looked at the woman with the sad brown eyes and black hair pulled into a braid wrapped around her head to form a crown. Her dark complexion was set off by the white lace around the collar of her light blue dress and the white bone buttons that ran down in a row to the waist. The tight sleeves were buttoned and had lace at each wrist and pearl ear bobs hung from small well-shaped ears. She seemed the perfect example of a young frontier woman except for the fact she was one hundred percent Apache.

"Please, call me Jessie. Ben acts as if he did it all himself and that William will grow up and become a carbon copy." Jessie reseated herself at the other cup of tea, now cold from having been left so long. She noticed a slight frown on the other young woman's face and placed her hand out to touch her arm.

"I'm sorry, did you lose a child? I'm afraid I don't know what to say around you, but if I misspeak you have only to tell me. I never mean to place anyone in an uncomfortable position, Mary," Jessie told the other woman honestly.

Mary grimaced and said just as honestly, "At least you are aware what you say may be uncomfortable for me. I have come to a conclusion I meet two types of women. Ones who ignore me and give me strange questioning stares behind my back and others who seem to find no question out of bounds. Including asking how many times I had been raped when I was a captive of the Comanche."

Jessie closed her eyes for a moment and then apologized. "I was unaware of your past circumstances, Mary. I knew you were an adopted child of the Reverend and Mrs. Burgess. I wasn't told of anything in your past. It wasn't brought up."

"The Reverend Burgess and his wife did adopt me, but only in the past three years. Before that, I spent much of my life as a captive living with the Comanche up north. I was very lucky to have been rescued and adopted into this fine Christian family." Mary spoke quietly, the way she did all things.

"You are aware of Emily's past history then, too? Is that why you are here?" Jessie wanted to make sure she understood the complicated relationships within this family.

"I am here for the reason you were told. There is an outbreak of measles in the town where my family lives and I am more susceptible than the others being Apache without any immunity to the disease. I am here, at this ranch, because being Apache and having been a

Comanche captive no one else would allow me in their homes no matter how civilized I make myself." There was a brittle smile on her lips. "It seems Christian charity does have its boundary."

"I see you are very hurt and rightfully so, Mary. It will take much longer, I think, before there will be peace between all the people in Texas. I was taken captive by the Comanche too, but was saved by my husband before anything cruel could happen to me." Jessie thought back to that day and then to her son in his cradle. "What I felt will haunt me, but little by little I am conquering it. I know it doesn't compare to what you went through. What I do know from my studies of aboriginal people is that time does lessen the pain and indignation eventually."

"Mrs. Edwards, I mean Emily, seems to have conquered her past, but then she is White and it must be easier to blend back into her family," Mary said, trying to regain her composure. She seemed to regret her earlier waspish words.

"I don't know. I've only been part of this family such a short time. The Major loves her and I think that is their salvation. I was told her own family did not take her back due to her first son, who was fathered by a Comanche chief." Jessie hoped she wasn't disclosing any family secrets, but Ben had told her earlier everyone knew about Morgan from the beginning.

"That must have been difficult. At least I did not get with child. One of the chief's older sisters had lost a daughter, the thirteen-year old had been getting water and had fallen into a fast-moving stream and drowned. It is said I resembled her and my new mother asked her brother if she could have me to replace her only child. I was given to her after a few days and then she protected me from the braves. I slept in her tent and learned to cook and take care of the buffalo hides and make clothes, just like all the other girls my age. She was very good to me in retrospect."

"May I ask how old you were?"

"I was about what you call eleven or twelve years old. The Comanche marry their girls off at about that age so I was saved from that by my mother. After six years I was rescued by the military. They were going to take me back to my band, but it had been wiped out years earlier. None of my family were left to claim me."

"You never wanted to stay with the Comanche, with your adoptive mother?" Jessie asked, knowing that often this happened, especially to members of other tribes.

"No, she was getting old and her brother was no longer a chief. I was past marrying age and it had been talked about at the tribal meetings that I should not be pampered so much. It was probably lucky the military found our band and took everyone to the fort and reservation. I was sent first to the missionary school where I studied to speak English. The Reverend and Mrs. Burgess saw me and thought I could be converted to Christianity and so I was. They are good people, but I am tired of being brought out and paraded in front of groups of contributors so they can see where their donations go. What good deeds come from saving the savages."

Jessie nodded in understanding at the sad younger woman. "Out of the frying pan into the fire…."

Mary seemed embarrassed. "I sound so ungrateful and I'm not. I appreciate all that the Burgess family and the church's congregation have done for me, but it gets tiring trying to smile and act White while looking Apache."

"I do understand and it will be kept between you and me. You have a very narrow tightrope to walk and I do not know how to help you. Possibly you can unburden yourself to Emily when she gets back from town. I'm sure she will have more insight than I do." Jessie stood to refill the teapot.

Jumping up, Mary put her arms out to protect Jessie yelling, "Take William and run, I'll hold him off."

Jessie turned in time to see the bread knife that had been on the table now in Mary's hand as she faced down the tall Comanche brave entering the kitchen, long tattoos down the calf of each leg, a breechcloth and moccasins his only covering in the summer heat. Mary was beginning to move forward, feigning jabbing movements to keep the warrior on guard.

Morgan, his right hand having gone instinctively to the hilt of his hunting knife on his hip, never stopped watching the eyes of his adversary but remained still.

"No, Mary, he's not an enemy. That's Morgan, my brother-in-law, he won't harm us, I promise." Jessie stepped between the two and then turned her back on Morgan to show Mary he really wasn't a danger to them.

Mary didn't move, still balanced on the balls of both feet, the knife menacingly pointed at Morgan.

Morgan took a more relaxed stance. "I just came in to find my mother. To let you know I was back for a few days, Little Sister, but I'll be in the tipi when she returns." He nodded politely towards Mary. "Nice to meet you." Then left as silently as he arrived.

Mary sat down as if her legs had gone out from under her, the knife shaking in her hand before Jessie took it from her. "I am sorry, Mary, I didn't know he was coming home. I thought you knew Emily's son visits here every few weeks when he's in Texas. He actually helped deliver William." At Mary's disbelieving expression Jessie continued, "There holding me up in his tipi right outside. I gave birth just like a Comanche squaw except Morgan was there for me and his nephew. Emily was my midwife."

"I-I didn't know. He looks so, so dangerous. I thought he was coming to kill the baby and take us as captives. I couldn't let him get William." Mary was still shaking a little as she spoke.

"Here, drink this tea with lots of sugar. You're still in shock." She watched as the other woman accepted the cup. "You were very brave, Mary, even though you hardly know me. You were going to sacrifice yourself to try to save me and William. I won't forget that, ever."

"I couldn't let him get the baby. You know what Comanche do to babies?" Mary turned to Jessie with large frightened eyes, remembering things best left forgotten.

"I do and I know what they do to their captives, yet you placed yourself in front of me, too. You are very strong and courageous, Mary. I hope you'll let me help you in any way I can." Jessie heard the buckboard pull around the house to the kitchen door. Emily was back from town and both young women needed her guidance.

At dinner that evening, a very debonair Morgan took his place at the dining room table. His hair pulled to the back of his neck with a colorful scrape of cloth, everything else was what a well-dressed man in Washington D. C. would wear for an evening event. He took the teasing from his stepfather and Ben with a smile and kept turning the conversation back to how the ranch was going and how much he had enjoyed the book by Jules Verne Jessie suggested he read.

Mary sat quietly beside Jessie and focused on her plate, taking small bites and chewing slowly. No one mentioned Mary's unfortunate confusion of that afternoon and if Jessie wasn't mistaken, Morgan's performance this evening was for Mary's benefit. Either trying to show her he was a very successful and educated man or at least not a savage.

Morgan never ate with the family in his Comanche dress, but this evening he had out did himself wearing eveningwear. Jessie was sure Morgan wanted to appear civilized to their guest, Mary. In fact, he rarely came into the house dressed as a brave unless it was to go right upstairs to change. But Jessie knew it is all he wore when visiting the Comanche or while staying in the tipi. He had told her it kept him grounded to his two worlds or he might forget one or the other.

After dinner, Ben challenged Morgan to a game of chess and the two men, so alike yet so different, sat down opposite each other and proceeded to make an evening of it, each one trying to outmaneuver the other. They called a stalemate when Jessie told the group she was going upstairs with William. Mary excused herself to do the same and hurried out of the room before anyone else.

Emily, holding a needle and thread over a new gown for William for when he grew too big for the infant sized ones they had both sewn, turned to her husband for information.

Waking her husband, she told him it was time to go to bed and he smiled as he always did when she said that. "I was just resting my eyes, love."

Jessie couldn't hold back a smile, knowing that she could see herself doing the same with Ben at some time in the future. Her husband winked at her then helped her stand with the baby in her arms.

Jessie, still awake and feeding William heard Morgan leave his room for the tipi a little while after everyone had become quiet. She wondered about Morgan's reasons for the flamboyant display this evening and knew it had to do with Mary and her reaction to him in his Comanche dress.

The next morning after breakfast, which Morgan ate in his tipi, Emily said, "Jessie, would you please speak with Morgan about an idea he's had. I'll watch William for you. Mary and I need to get acquainted, anyway, and this is a good time."

"Certainly Emily, call out if he gets too fussy or hungry." She knew her mother-in-law liked to carry William around with her as the Comanche mothers did.

Morgan was in the tipi with the flap wide open and the bottom of the hides rolled up to let the breeze in funneling up and out through the smoke vent.

"You wanted to speak with me, Morgan?"

"An idea I had, Little Sister. I know you and Ben plan on spending the next few months here and I was wondering if you would chronicle the Numunuu people as they are now, before we have to alter our lifestyle even more, lose any more of our culture and language."

This wasn't what Jessie had expected this conversation to be about. She thought it might have to do with Mary but not a job request. Her first instinct was to tell him no. That she couldn't face the people who had abducted her and Ben. Who had done so much harm to Ben with so much violence. Before she voiced her refusal the thought that if she couldn't face these people here in the safety of her family, how would she ever be able to face any group alone?

"I could do as much as I can until we leave next spring. That's when Ben and I decided we could best travel with William. But I don't do languages, there are specialists who work with the different dialects. I only know the Comanche travelled south from the Shoshone of the Great Plains."

"I know it's a big undertaking and I wouldn't ask it of you, but one of the younger boys, just entering manhood, asked me what it was like to follow a buffalo herd. How did we kill so many buffalo to make all the tipis for his band, yet, he's seen so few live ones in his life. It was difficult to explain how big those herds once were and how many horses were owned by the Numunuu. They were in the tens of thousands at one time."

She began to understand how much must have changed for him in the last decade. "I can study the more peaceful bands close to here without too much trouble. Ben will want to accompany me and I could use him as an interpreter. I would like to commission a photographer to come here to take photos of how your people are dressed and living now." She began to get intrigued with the idea and how she could best save the information she had as it transformed right in front of her.

145

"I'll take you, at least the first time so there will be no mistakes as to who they will answer to if anyone tries anything. I will claim you and William as family in front of the tribe. They already know Ben as one of us."

"I've never asked Ben much about his becoming a Comanche," Jessie said as she watched Morgan's face.

"It was long ago, before I was very well known among the tribes. I had been back with my people, but some of them still looked at me with distrust since I had lived with the Whites for so long. I did my best for Ben and he lived. That is all I can take credit for because they damn near killed him. It seems like a life time ago and yet it wasn't. For the Comanche so much has changed, chiefs murdered, treaties signed and then signed again. The Texas Rangers were created to bring the Numunuu under control and that occurred during the last few decades." He seemed to realize how vulnerable his people had become.

"I'll get as much of the truth and history as I can, I promise. Emily can be of help and even, Mary." At her name Jessie saw a flare of something in Morgan's dark eyes.

"Let me know when you want me to introduce you and I'll take you over. I only planned on being here a couple of days so returning to the tribe for a visit won't be a hardship."

Ben wasn't as encouraging as Jessie thought he would be. He didn't trust some of the elders, knowing they had no control over the younger braves, and allowed the braves to do whatever they wanted. Finally, he told her he would go with her, but she would remain with him at all times. She wasn't to be out of his sight.

Emily kept her own counsel when Morgan mentioned his request at dinner that evening. Mary didn't contribute an opinion one way or another remaining quiet as she usually did when the men were present. As the room became silent after the announcement, Emily pointed out a drawing of William that was so lifelike it was better than a photograph.

With pride in her voice, Emily said excitedly, "We have an artist in our midst and didn't realize it. Mary drew a portrait of William for me this afternoon. She captured his little baby smile perfectly and I am sure that wasn't easy. He doesn't stay still for very long at a time unless he's sleeping."

Jessie asked, "Oh, may I see it? I can draw plants and insects, but when it comes to portraits and such, I become all thumbs. They never come out resembling the person at all. I so wanted to catch William at this age, before he lost all that baby pudge and began talking and running around."

Emily brought in an already framed and glassed pencil drawing looking exactly like William laughing up into his mother's face his eyes alight with mischief already. "Oh, Mary, this is perfect, even a camera couldn't have caught this pose, his look. I must beg you to do one more before you need to leave us."

Mary, seeming pleased she had been able to repay her hosts for their kind welcome, was also humbled. "My talent has been less than appreciated by my adopted family. They told me I was wasting God's time. That I should spend that time in contemplative thoughts and winning converts over to the church." She looked down shyly. "I simply draw what I see. I don't have any kind of real knowledge of art."

147

Morgan's strong voice asked over the other's denial of Mary's comment. "What if I hired you to make drawings of the Numunuu and pay you for doing so as I've hired Jessie? I also think I can get a newspaper in Washington to pick them up for a series of articles they will be doing on the loss of the aboriginal peoples of North America."

Everyone immediately became quiet and turned to Mary for her answer to such an unusual request, especially if one thought about Mary's history with the Comanche and being of an aboriginal people almost driven to extinction by another.

"I would have to write and get permission to do so from my family. I was only supposed to be here a few weeks until the measles had run their course in town," she answered quietly, not looking at anyone at the table.

"You are more than welcome to stay either way, Mary. It's nice to have another woman to talk with since Jessie and I are usually outnumbered," Emily offered the young woman, whom the family had grown fond of since accepting her into their home.

"I'll write a letter to the Reverend and Mrs. Burgess tonight and ask if I might stay a little longer," she said quietly, still staring at the tablecloth rather than the faces around the table.

"That will work out well since I'm going in to town tomorrow. I'll mail it for you." Morgan smiled since everything seemed settled to his satisfaction.

The meal ended with everyone trying to figure out the logistics of getting Jessie to the Comanche camp outside of town. Possibly Ben taking her while staying as protection and interpreter and keeping William close by to be fed.

At first Emily volunteered to go and watch the baby, but everyone in her family knew she didn't like to be near that many Comanche. So, Mary said she could stay with William and draw when Jessie or Ben had the baby. Morgan stayed out of this conversation, letting the ones most involved work out their separate roles.

CHAPTER NINE

The Reverend Burgess gave his blessing for Mary to stay and work with the Comanche, writing that he hoped she would use her time wisely. She was to tell the heathens of the Lord God and his Son reminding Mary she was given this great opportunity to spread the word.

Emily, when given the letter to read, was amazed at the Reverend's complete lack of understanding of the people he intended to convert. Reading the Bible to them would not make a Christian, even though the Comanche were losing faith in their old spirits and turning to peyote to form new cultural relationships.

The small group set out after a few days like a wagon train heading over the Cumberland Gap trail. The women and William with Ben driving were in the buggy, a buckboard stocked with everything Emily felt would be needed and then things that might come in handy following them. Morgan, on his pinto pony, rode bareback in front wearing his buckskin breechcloth and moccasins.

The entourage arrived at the Comanche encampment and many of the Numunuu walked toward the group, staring at the newcomers who had driven in of their own free will and not as captives. Since this was a band from Morgan's original tribe, they were familiar with both him and Ben, although they did not look at Ben with the same respect they did Morgan.

As one of the chiefs, Morgan told the surrounding group in their own language what the interlopers were doing in the village with his blessing. The stoic faces were undecipherable and Jessie didn't know if she were going to be able to interview any of the tribe or have to return to the ranch with her quest unfulfilled.

Morgan explained to Jessie, "I have made arrangements for several of the elders to speak with you first. To give you a history of my people. They thought they should go first in case they died before they got to tell you their stories."

"So there are some who have already agreed to speak with me? I thought you were up against a brick wall here."

"They want to get the history down before it is lost. They complain the younger generation does not appreciate all that was done before them. The young braves complain the elders are too old and feeble and won't fight, won't go off the reservation and tell the Whiteman and the Army to leave them live as they always have lived." He shook his head a little before continuing, "The young don't know it's too late for that. When the buffalo were killed off it was the Numunuu that died. A small band can live off the land for a year or two, but then they end up eating their horses so they don't starve. Their children will not thrive and their women will become weak, too weak to bear children."

He looked over to the squaws watching, waiting for instructions from the chiefs. "They live on the tales they have heard all their lives around the fires of the elders. That the Numunuu were a chosen people, a people blessed by the gods, a people to be feared by all others and they want it to be true again. They are so sure it can be true again and then there are the rest of us who know that way of life is gone forever. That is what I want written down before the men who lived that life are all dead and their memories lost."

"If they'll tell me, I will make sure it's written and saved in the archives of the Smithsonian for posterity. All of our history, whether pleasant or not, needs to be honestly recorded so centuries from now Americans will know how their country was formed and who made up its people."

"I will introduce you to White Snake and then come back and stay with Mary and William, help set up their shade for the day. Mary seems a little frightened and possibly having me around will make her more at ease among the others." He gazed at the young woman clutching William to her breasts as if the Comanche were going to snatch him from her at any moment.

"Perhaps we shouldn't have brought her. I don't want her sitting here prettified the whole time," Jessie said worriedly.

"I'll remain with her. You won't have to worry about William or Mary."

Ben added to his brother, "That may be what she's afraid of. You don't exactly exude trust to Mary in that outfit." He looked pointedly at the large bowie knife on Morgan's hip.

Morgan looked pointedly at the gun and holster at Ben's hip. "How much talking did you think I had to do to get them to accept you into their midst? They know you're a Ranger."

"Ex-Ranger," Ben said through gritted teeth.

"There's no such thing as an ex-Ranger and you know it. Let's agree we have a lot of distrustful people here and they all have reason to be. Now let us get Jessie settled with White Snake and I'll come back and charm Mary." Morgan walked toward an old man wrapped in a blanket even in the heat of the Texas summer day.

White Snake was even older than he appeared, remembering his father telling him of driving the Apache southward across the Rio del Fierro and finally into Mexico. He told, no bragged, *"The number of horses owned by the Numunuu in the Comancheria, the lands the Texans and others allotted to my people, so many horses they were counted in the millions, numbers unknown to the other tribes. The Numunuu's wealth was worth more than the gold the Whiteman hunted for or the land the farmers came for. Numunuu's wealth was in horses which increased in number yearly and in bison which roamed freely giving the Numunuu everything we needed, given to us by benevolent gods who also taught us how to defend that wealth, protect our people and way of life."*

Jessie's fingers were cramping from writing her notes so quickly to keep up with the old man's stories, depending on spelling Comanche words by sounding them out. She would ask Ben to help her later, when she would rewrite the notes into something more readable. Then she would collate this man's stories with those of other tribal members until there was one continuous history of the Numunuu people just as Morgan wanted.

Returning to the wagon, she found Mary drawing the scene outside her little hiding area. Morgan wasn't far away giving Mary her breathing room, but letting her know he was protecting her and William.

"How was he?" Jessie asked, going over to the cradle and looking down at her son, loving him so much it hurt.

"I think he got fussy because he was hungry, but then I rocked him and he fell asleep. I would have sent for you if he had become upset or cried." Mary placed the sketchpad down, the scene of the encampment captured right down to the bone scrapers hanging outside a tipi.

"Let's have that picnic Emily sent with us and if William hasn't woken up by then I'll wake him and feed him before I take another interview. There is a lot more information to cover than I thought. These elders kept everything they ever heard to pass on to the following generation and the next. It will be fascinating to hear about the Numunuu's early days, before the Whiteman came." Jessie opened the basket and set on one of the stools Emily insisted on sending along with the table.

Ben joined them under the canvas covering. "I was unaware of some of that history. Do you think it's all true?" Taking the plate, she prepared for him and the cup of lemonade poured from the jars accompanying the food, he leaned against the side of the wagon.

She gave Mary a plate and then got one for herself, waiting for Morgan to come and get one too or perhaps he didn't want to let his band see him eat like a Whiteman with fork and plate, two items she learned the Numunuu didn't bother with.

Morgan did finally come, but took the chicken with his hands and ate the meat off the bone, facing inward, squatting on his haunches with his back to the outside world.

Handing him the rest of the jar of lemonade he drank right from the rim, finishing it in one long swallow. She smiled at his ability to slip into the Comanche customs so easily. "Did you want me to do another interview after I've fed William or do you want us to go back to the ranch?"

"If you're not too tired, I think taking another interview would be fine. The elders seem to accept you and Ben without any problems and they love to tell their stories. Most of the rest of us have heard them many times." He hesitated and turned to the young woman completely ignoring his presence. "Are you all right staying here a few more hours, Mary? I know it's probably difficult for you."

Mary swallowed the food she had been chewing and as always said quietly, "I am fine. William and I are enjoying our time together."

Morgan took that as an affirmative to her staying and went back out to sit among his people, speaking quietly with men who came and went during the afternoon. Mary continued drawing and William played then napped and woke again. Mary took care of his needs as they arose Jessie noticed from where she sat with an elder medicine man.

The group headed back to the ranch after taking a few minutes to pack up. Morgan stayed at the encampment and didn't show for dinner that night. The rest were tired from their busier than usual day, even William, although he had the opportunity to nap. Mary went to her room right after helping with the dishes as she always did and Jessie and Ben went to their room with William to have some quiet time as a family.

Emily had another meal packed up for the group the next day. Morgan came out of his tipi as the buggy and buckboard pulled up to the kitchen door and the day repeated the one that had come before. After a few days of talking with the elders, Jessie tracked down Morgan who was usually around the compound and asked to speak with him.

"I need to speak with the women. The older women, if possible, since they will know the most about how things were done before there were metal implements traded for with the Spanish." She showed him the sheets of paper covered in writing and small drawings. "I have enough of the battles and history of the travels for now I think."

Morgan hesitated then told her honestly, "The women are being more difficult than I thought they would be. They don't want their knowledge passed out of the tribe. They feel they have centuries into learning their skills to tan the buffalo and sew the tipis. They can set up or take down a camp in twenty minutes and they take great pride in that. They don't want others learning their methods."

"Well, you can explain to them I only write in English and then all this information will be stored in the Whiteman's capital in Washington D. C. The Numunuu's enemies will not have easy access to the information. And they don't have to tell me anything they think is too secretive, but there are no longer bison to tan so passing on that information will not be revealing anything to anyone any longer." Jessie hoped giving him some weapons of words to use would soften the women to speak with her.

"I will try one more time, but it is not worth getting the squaws upset. They are more determined and more dangerous than the braves. We are afraid of them even though the elders pretend that they are the ones in control," Morgan admitted as he helped pack up the buckboard again.

Morgan must have talked fast because when the group got to the encampment there were three squaws waiting to tell their stories to Jessie. She thought if she brought William to the meeting, he would break the ice and he did. He gave the squaws his wide toothless grin, drool slipping past the side of his mouth and making the metal shaker in his hand slick as he sucked on it. When he pulled at his mother's blouse, she suckled him to the nodding approval of the older women. Ben had trouble keeping up with their often over lapping voices, explaining how to raise a healthy brave and train a girl into being a good wife and mother.

One of the oldest women remembered collecting the poles for the tipis. *I remember as a child my mother cutting and then stripping off the bark and limbs. The camp was by the banks of the Cimarron River and the women were making travois to carry all of their belongings to the next spot where the braves had made a kill.*

The other women also told of moving quickly when the braves had made a bison kill, tearing down and moving a whole village in less than an hour, following the brave's trails and getting there in time to start working the hides and cutting the meat up for each families' use.

Some of the women had brought the sharp bone scrappers and sewing needles used to make the tipi coverings. *"I remember the big tipis that housed the elders' meetings where all braves were allowed to speak, where chiefs and war chiefs were selected and decisions for the tribes were made. The women were proud. Some of these tipis were used when the Numunuu were at their greatest numbers. Took as many as twenty-two hides, hides that had to be scrapped on both sides by the women, removing the long thick hair of the buffalo using fire ash in water. Then the squaws washed and worked the hides until they were soft and supple while finally smoking them over a fire, leaving the hides a light tan color with a permanent odor of wood smoke to them."*

Jessie asked about the travois because she used one to bring Ben back to their camp after he was so badly wounded. The squaws were in charge of making them and loading them, making the unloading at the next stop easier as they had to put the tipis up again. They told of constructing the beds that kept them up off the cold winter ground and then covering them with bison robes.

Jessie was amazed at how much of the Numunuu's implements, household goods and clothing were based on the buffalo, the horns for drinking vessels and scoops and ladles. The bison's stomach used to carry and store water, the brains and liver used to process the hides or used on their hair like pomade or as a medicinal salve, its sinew and gut used for bow strings. Bone and horn shaped into arrow heads. There were no metal implements until after the Numunuu traded with the Mexicans for horses that were broken to saddle by the younger braves.

One of the squaws brought out knee high boots that are used when the weather is cold and snow covers the ground. Others showed off the fine bead work used to decorate the clothing used during celebrations and feasts. Jessie was impressed with the quality of the workmanship knowing how primitive their tools were, the needles made of bone and horn. Most pieces of clothing were tied on with strips of bison leather.

Jessie met with these women for several days in a row, seeing Mary draw the squaws and their dress while Jessie had William with her.

Ben said, "I'm very proud of you, how you can write and ask questions without showing any bias or indication of your personal opinions. You accept the squaws' stories and their talk of the captives. How they were treated and viewed in the same way as they accepted the dogs that followed the camps eating scraps from the bison carcasses." He watched her eyes. "You also took in stride the truth these dogs were eaten when other game became scarce as were horses in the really lean years. At least no one said they had eaten a captive, which might have been the end of your research right then and there."

One of the braves Jessie interviewed was a captive who had accepted the Numunuu as his own, going through the dangerous and painful rites to become a warrior. He spoke of accompanying the raiding parties and taking captives as well as killing settlers and burning their homes and barns.

Jessie wrote with shaking fingers as Ben described in English the grisly details of one raid by the Comanche on a small settlement of White settlers along the Red River. The cutting off of the genitals of the men and stuffing them into their mouths while the squaws sewed their mouths closed, all before the real torture began. Then the cutting of flesh and the burning alive until death finally brought them peace. In some cases, even death didn't stop the mutilation. Mostly the squaws taking pleasure in making even the corpses unrecognizable.

Jessie was close to vomiting when Ben cut the interview short, helping his wife up and over to the wagon before she was sick in front of the elders. He knew he should have stopped interpreting when he saw how pale she had gotten. They would need to have a conversation about just how much of the truth she could hear, how much he would tell her before he felt it was too gruesome, even to be chronicled for posterity.

Jessie skipped dinner that evening and the meal was quiet as everyone made an early night. In their bedroom, Ben had a quiet talk with his wife, trying not to bring up the actual words of that afternoon's interview. "Honey, I didn't like the way conversations went today. I want to let you know I won't translate anything so sinister again. I don't want it tainting our relationship and what we have now. I might add stories to your work if I think it worth writing, but otherwise some of the eviler Comanche attacks may be lost to history. There are enough graphic details out there already."

Jessie reluctantly agreed and hugged her husband as they lay on the bed. "I'm just glad Nathan will be here tomorrow. I know he'll start right in with taking photographs and will get my mind off those grizzly tales. I want to make sure he gets the little girls with their buckskin dolls. Did you know they sew all the clothes for those dolls themselves? They are really very good for that age. There's even bead work and fringe of deer fur on the little dresses."

Ben held his wife to his side. "Yes, I did know. They make them exactly like they will have to when they get married. Now get some rest. I am very interested in this

Nathan Fontaine. And are there any surprises for me? Like did he share a tent with you, too?" he asked teasing.

When Jessie became quiet Ben said accusingly, "He did. You and he shared a tent?"

"With my father and three Sherpa. It was a necessity to keep us from freezing. We were all bundled up and lying like logs in a hearth," Jessie told her husband, while seemingly trying to judge how upset he might be. Jessie didn't want Ben and Nathan to get off on the wrong foot right from the start.

"No nudging involved?" he asked back to his teasing way.

"No nudging involved. My relationship with Nathan isn't that kind," she told him as he settled for the night again.

But Ben didn't fall right to sleep. He lay next to Jessie and wondered if she knew what kind of a relationship Nathan Fontaine had wanted from her back then. She hadn't discerned his interest in her as he waited until they were both free of the university's study she was in the Texas desert that first time. She knew about the act, but not the mysteries between a man and woman. Ben wondered if Jessie had explained she was married now and if she hadn't, was that the reason Fontaine high-tailed it down to Texas from the east coast so quickly?

CHAPTER TEN

Jessie seemed excited as she got ready to go to the Comanche camp. Their buckboard was going on into town to bring Nathan back from where the stagecoach dropped him and his equipment off. The group all rode in the wagon, leaving the buggy at the ranch. It was less cumbersome and not as intimidating to the tribe as they entered their village.

Ben didn't want to interview the old warriors again so soon, knowing they would again describe the culmination of every battle. He wanted to speak with the present medicine man, getting Jessie more insight in the peyote religion that was becoming more and more important to the Comanche tribes. Ben dressed as any Texas rancher, tan shirt and trousers, a bandana around his neck and knee boots with pointed toes. He carried a side arm in a holster on a belt and ten-gallon hat on his head. So far, he had been accepted at every interview, even the ones where childbirth was discussed.

Going first to the tent of the medicine man, the old man had Ben come into the shade of the tipi, the bottom rolled up a foot or so from the ground to allow the air to come in and up through the open flap at the tip of the hide covering keeping the tipi cooler.

The elderly wiseman, his grey hair parted down the middle and a bright red clay dye on his scalp, sat in the center of the tipi on a buffalo robe. His braids were wrapped in decorative rabbit fur and placed over each shoulder to lay on his chest tattooed with geometric designs. His loin cloth and moccasins the only covering except for the chest plate of bone and beads.

"Younger Brother of Toshawi, I have been waiting for you to come to me. You seem worried and I do not see a reason for your concern," the older man said, recognizing Ben as many of the younger Comanche hadn't. As Morgan's or rather White Knife's younger brother.

"I was wondering if anyone was still here who would recognize me or would remember from so many years ago. I do not follow the Comanche warrior code so use my English name of Edwards," he said, not committing himself to any Comanche control.

"If you no longer wore the White's clothes your scars of manhood would show and you could walk among us unscathed," the medicine man informed him.

Ben gave a smile. "Not exactly. I was captured by a raiding party about ten months ago and I don't think they were welcoming me back into the Numunuu community." He sat cross legged on the hard dirt so he was on the same level as the medicine man.

"I remember how hard Toshawi, White Knife, fought for your life, telling the others that as he was your brother then you were their brother as well. It would have been easier if Ten Bears did not want the same squaw to take as wife. Your brother was going to bring the horses he had to offer and Ten Bears did not have as many. Your brother offered to turn away and let Ten Bears have the squaw. That is how he won the votes to save your life and allow you to pass the tests to become a warrior instead."

163

Ben felt his brows lower and he thought about that time, a time he wanted to forget once he had escaped the warriors who inflicted such pain. Even to the point of forgetting what his brother had endured right beside him.

The old man nodded as he remembered. "Toshawi told them he would go through the same tests they gave to you to ensure they were not going to merely kill you with the tasks. White Knife knew they would not dare kill him outright. His father's family were too strong and would require vengeance if he died," the old man explained to Ben of what happened more than twelve years earlier after Ben had been captured and almost killed by a raiding party.

Ben remembered Morgan interrupting the torture and the next thing Ben knew he was in the middle of becoming a warrior standing next to his brother.

"What happened to the young woman? Did Ten Bears marry her?" he asked, wondering why Morgan had never told him the rest of the story.

"Ten Bears moved her to another tribe that his mother was from and she gave him two sons and a daughter before he was killed in battle with the Kiowa Apache. Ten Bears moved because he did not trust his wife to remain faithful, even though your brother promised never to touch her."

"Did she return to this tribe after Ten Bears' death? Does my brother know she's free to marry again?" he asked, needing to know how much his brother paid for Ben's freedom.

"She stayed so that her sons could learn from their grandfather as it should be. White Knife knows, but he made a promise. It was not bound by life or death. It was a promise. He will not go to her or seek her out. This is an honor that must be held to," the medicine man said emphatically.

"It cost him a lot more than I realized to save me. I should show more gratitude although my becoming a warrior didn't seem to have saved me from much when I was taken in the raid last fall."

"The younger generation are too hot headed to listen to the elders and chiefs, to those members who have lived the years of change. The life of the Numunuu will never be the same again. The great herds are gone, moved on to other lands where we cannot follow," he said, telling Ben what he already knew.

Ben felt he could be truthful with this man. "It is worse than that. The bison are all but gone, not only here, all over the Great Plains. The Shoshone up north have none to hunt, either. The settlers are fencing off the land to farm or graze cattle. I wasn't sure how many of the Comanche realized they would need to change their life or parish."

"It is good then that I am old and will soon leave this world, one that is changing too fast. We came from farmers in the north and then the gods gave us horses. Then we were given the open spaces of the Comancheria and the bison and now everything seems to be taken away. We are faced again to become farmers on the land the Whiteman has allowed us, but this too shall be taken away. I do not know what the Numunuu did to anger the gods, but we may not live through the wrath sent down to us."

Both men sat silently staring out the open tipi flap.

A wagon pulled into view and a man jumped down. Lifting Jessie off the ground, he swung her around. Ben could hear her laughing happily. His mouth turned down as he tried to believe his wife's words of the night before, 'our relationship is not of that kind'.

"Ah-h-h," said the old man looking between the couple outside and the man sitting next to him. "You worry your woman may be interested in this other man even though she has given you a son. This is only the uncertainty of a young husband. She is not attracted to this man. I know this for certain." Then he waited and added, "I will call her Laughing Waters because she sounds like the bubbling brook. Tell your woman I will speak with her about the Numunuu and how we used to rule the lands."

"I will let her know. She will probably want a photograph of such a wise man as yourself. Will that be allowed?" Ben asked, and got a nod of approval for this request.

Walking toward the couple still standing too close together, he listened to the sound of his wife's laughter, a sound he hadn't heard much of the last few months. Maybe she wasn't as happy and content as he thought she was. He would have to find a way to make her want to stay with him as a family. Having this interloper come in from the exciting outside world, reminding Jessie of far off continents wasn't exactly going to help matters.

Ben put out his hand as he approached. "This must be Nathan Fontaine. I'm glad you made it out here in such good time. I just got the medicine man's approval for his photograph to be taken." He looked into the face of a Negro ex-slave with sherry brown eyes and black hair cut close to his scalp. His skin was smooth and the color of coffee with cream, bright white, even teeth shown from a wide friendly smile.

"I'm glad to meet you, too. I wanted to see the man who had captured Jessie's heart," he said honestly, studying the man in front of him.

"That would be William, our son over under the canvass. He always sleeps about now, but will be yelling for his supper anytime," Ben answered him in a friendly manner. After all Ben could be generous seeing as Jessie and William were his.

"I'll take several photographs of the baby, too. So, you can show him how little he started off at," Nathan offered readily.

"Well, we have some wonderful drawings of him. Mary, our friend who has been doing the sketches I told you about, is excellent at doing portraitures, too." Jessie walked Nathan toward the shade they had set up for William and introduced the two artists.

"Mary has been a God-send for us. I would never have nearly as much done if she hadn't volunteered to take care of William and do the sketches. Look them over. She is so detailed and really catches the mood of the subject. I don't know how she does it, but they are going to be a great addition to the history book. She has been doing the front and back of head pieces and clothing, showing how they were cut out and sewn. Look at the beading work on some of these newer pieces and the jewelry of bone and shells," Jessie enthused to Mary's embarrassment.

Ben noted Nathan, an artist himself, knew the delicate lines indicated a steady hand and an eye to detail that isn't often found in an amateur, especially an Apache female. Nathan smiled at Mary and complimented her again. Watching, Ben noted the high color in her cheeks.

167

The group had an alfresco meal and Nathan unpacked his gear including the chemicals he would need to get the negatives safely on the glass plates. Jessie helped him, moving in unison, knowing what the other was going to take or move with the long practice of working together. Ben watched as he held William, but he didn't pay as much attention to the sleeping infant as he usually did. His mind kept going back to Jessie's insistence she and Nathan weren't that close. Ben was beginning to think Nathan thought differently.

The larger group packed at the end of their day and headed back to the ranch. Nathan sat in the back with Mary and Jessie while Ben and the driver sat on the bench seat, talking together. The three adults bounced along while Nathan filled Jessie in on the trip he had recently returned from to the Amazon basin.

"It is fascinating, but even I was a little frightened of their use of poisoned arrows and the shrinking of heads. Too much like the voodoo of the bayous. I have much more respect for those who travel there and live to tell about it. Leeches the size of armadillos, mosquitoes and blood sucking bats, both the same size," he laughed as Mary's eyes kept getting bigger and bigger as she listened to him.

Jessie slapped his shoulder reprimanding him, "Now stop that talk. You're scaring us on purpose." Although Jessie didn't seem frightened at all.

"I'm sorry, I'm trying to impress you with my bravery and skill although they used those machete type knives to much more advantage than I could my fencing sword," he teased, trying to get the ladies to forget the more gruesome thoughts.

"No one to fence with, I take it? Perhaps I should try my hand at it again," Jessie said as she eyed the long case lying next to them, probably holding his sword and saber.

"No, *ma Cherie*, please leave me with some semblance of dignity. You about took me down the last time we were adversaries. I think I'll keep from being unmanned and play a game of chess or cards to appease your competitive nature," he said, smiling at her, his eyes bright with love. Ben made note that his wife and that man had an easy camaraderie that only months together could forge. Ben needed to remind Jessie that at one time they had had that kind of a relationship, in the tent as they worked together before the Comanche turned her life upside-down.

Emily met the group and graciously extended the welcome to Nathan to her home. Negros weren't unknown in the Rangers, but most weren't invited to stay in the home of a Major. He knew Nathan wouldn't be treated any differently as Ben helped haul the photographer's gear up to one of the vacant bedrooms. The two younger women offered to help Emily with the meal and as usual were turned down and told to go rest or get ready. Jessie usually took this time to feed William so he would either sleep or stay quiet during dinner. Right after the evening meal, his grandmother held him whether he was asleep or awake, getting in her time with the baby before Jessie took him up to bed with her.

They all opted for an early night, each for their own reasons. Nathan was tired from travelling without a break. Emily and the Major wanted to spend time alone while Mary wished to escape the chance of Morgan returning home. Jessie took care of William and would give him his final feeding for the night and Ben needed to try to figure out how to get Jessie closer to him again.

Since the baby, Ben had been sleeping in the same room, the same bed as Jessie, but they hadn't discussed being intimate. Ben wasn't sure this was the right time, but the baby was over two months old and some discrete questions to his mother let him know it could happen if Jessie wanted it to.

The point was moot though as he saw how tired Jessie was as she finally got William fed and lying in the cradle beside the bed. Ben would have to be content with the fact Jessie let him hold her to his body and didn't push his hands away when she found them cradling her breast in the morning. He kissed her shoulder and accepted what he had. At least she was still here with him in Texas. He would owe Morgan another favor for keeping Jessie here. He would add it to his list of saving his life more than once.

The next day Morgan was back, wearing a Comanche chief's paint and head dress as Jessie had asked so Nathan could take a photograph of him from several angles. Morgan knew it was to chronicle his clothing and had made sure everything was authentic to his title and tribe. Not that chiefs wore different clothing, but some tribal members were accepting the clothes of the Whiteman. Wearing shirts and hats, especially if they had worked with the military to go with their loin cloths and leggings. Morgan wore the fringed leggings even though it was still midsummer. He had also laid out a buffalo robe to wear as Nathan posed him in front of the tipi.

"I usually like to photograph people as I see them, but I realize your people are changing, getting assimilated into other cultures," he told Morgan as he made sure the feather headdress showed to its best, catching the bright morning light.

"It had to be that or die fighting. There aren't any other choices now. It has all gone on too long and my people have to adapt or perish. I take it you have studied other people who have come to an end?" Morgan asked.

"I am afraid so. Usually it is the less warrior-like people who get adopted into another, taken over by brute strength. But the American Indians have been disappearing since the Whiteman came to North America bringing with him an alluring way of living and a tempting non-violent method of over-coming resistance," he said. "All right, hold that pose for a moment." Then a flash of powder went off in the wood holder held high in the air.

"So, you blame our loss of culture on the Whiteman?" Morgan asked as he moved to where Nathan pointed him, picking up the heavy buffalo robe.

"Not all of it. There could have been more give and take on both sides and things might have worked out better. The aboriginal people wanted, coveted, much of the Whiteman's material goods and his women and his God and his knowledge. The first Natives went willingly with Columbus back to Europe and many of the earlier travelers liked what they found in Spain and Holland and England. The coveting of those things brought their own form of slavery and gave the Whiteman dominance over the rest of us."

"Are you saying this because you were once a slave yourself?" Morgan asked.

"I never felt I was a slave. I was raised in the plantation house with my mother sleeping in the master's bed every night. I was educated through university, taught to waltz, fence and shoot, speak three languages plus the Creole dialect. I can ride like a Prussian, fence like a Frenchman, shoot like a Kentuckian and throw a Bowie knife like a Canadian fur trapper. I owe all this to my French White father who had no legitimate off-spring so he raised me to be his heir, but the war came up and ended all that for me. I am now a free man," he said sarcastically.

"I thought you had been a slave, sorry for the misunderstanding," Morgan said, moving his arm to have the leather band tied on his bicep show as well as the geometric tattoo and colorful breast plate.

"I was as was my mother. My father owned me and my mother and my aunt. He liked owning slaves and he wouldn't have it any other way. I was sent to fight for the South, my regiment of other unhappy Negro southerners right beside me, not liking having to take orders from a man like me. My Lieutenant was an uneducated share cropper who could hardly shoot straight since he was drunk most of the time. Most of my comrades at arms were killed within the first month of fighting," Nathan said as he stepped behind the camera and the photo was taken, saved for posterity.

"Was there something between you and Jessie then, at one time?" Morgan needed to know since he knew his younger brother was concerned and didn't want any more surprises to his family.

"You and I are alike in this matter. Our heritage, our culture is split. We belong to two or none depending on how you view things. I would be beaten, hung, drawn and quartered depending on who I became interested in. I would assume it's pretty much the same for you. Our wives would be ridiculed and humiliated and defenseless in society, not fish nor fowl, I think my French ancestors would call it. I am not only a man without a country, I am a man without a culture. I'm not sure which is worse."

Morgan held his pose as he was told and admitted that much of what Nathan said was true for both of them. Even the Comanche never fully accepted a captive, there were always those who held the captives' original lives against them.

CHAPTER ELEVEN

Mary stayed in the house, helping Emily in the kitchen since both Ben and Jessie were caring for William. Her gaze kept moving to the outside, to where Nathan and Morgan were taking the photographs. Mary tried to convince herself that she was interested in the process, of how Nathan posed then took each photograph, but she knew her gaze was on Morgan more than Nathan. She noted his strong back muscles and biceps emphasized by the tattoos and leather bands.

Then he stood and shifted the buffalo robe, holding it off one shoulder, allowing the chest plate and braid with the colorful scrap of material and single feather to show. She watched as he removed the leggings exposing the strong muscular legs, the calves decorated with geometric designs from knee to heel and his thighs thick and hairless. Her fingers itched to catch the beauty of this man's body, even his scars which seemed to be many were beautiful to her. Mary began to wipe the plates with more energy than necessary, afraid of what her interest actually meant.

Jessie came downstairs saying, "Ben wants me to have a break. Told me to do anything I want, but that was what I was doing. I was having a lazy day, how about you? You need to do anything here at home?"

"Me? No, I was just helping Emily since there are getting to be so many of us for meals and such. I cooked most of the meals for my family so it isn't so much different if I cook here. There's more variety here, of course. The Burgess have a limited budget and a lot of mouths to feed. They are always taking in more so this place is like home in that way, too."

"I was paging through your sketch pad." At the statement, Mary began re-wiping the already dry plates as Jessie added, "I hope that was all right with you."

Mary didn't meet Jessie's gaze but said, "Of course, I told you to look at them anytime. Let me know if I'm getting what you need for your chronicles."

"I think they're all wonderful, detailed and excellent contents for what we're trying to do. I was going to show Morgan because he is basically paying for this study, but I think some of these are personal, like the ones of William and Ben and me." Jessie noted the other woman seemed to appear guilty.

"I simply drew what I saw. I'm not an artist. More of a sketcher who makes copies of what is there. I don't have anything to do with content," she said humility in her voice.

"I'm not an artist, Mary. I merely sketch the plants and note their colors. You are an artist, taking everyday things and finding the beauty in them. I particularly enjoyed seeing Morgan in hardly more than what Mother Nature ensured him. He's a beautiful male specimen." Jessie sighed dramatically, fanning her face with her open hand like some southern belle.

Mary dropped her head and laughed, actually laughed for the first time in Jessie's hearing. "But he's your brother-in-law. How can you talk like that about kin?"

"I may be married, but I'm not blind. I am glad there are certain aspects that seem to run in the family, but I can enjoy a handsome male as well as the next woman. We're lucky we get to look as much as we want. You could do more if you wished to. I know Morgan isn't immune to your beauty, either," Jessie told the now beet-red young woman watching the object of their conversation through the window.

Mary giggled continuing to watch out the window, seemingly allowing her imagination to roam as she unabashedly soaked up Morgan's every move.

"Are they almost done yet? Or do we have time to go out and pretend we want another pose or different clothes?" Jessie asked, stretching to watch the two men.

"What are you two doing, I heard you giggling all the way upstairs," said the raspy voice of her husband making both women jump as if caught with their hands in the cookie jar. They turned and faced him, guilt written all over both their faces, she was sure.

Jessie regained her composure first saying, "We were discussing humanity. I thought you were going to take a nap with William," she said as if she had nothing to hide.

He glanced at both women before saying, "We've decided to take a walk. William's never been out to the stable. I'm going to introduce him to a few of the regulars."

"That sounds nice even if he's a year or so young for the outing. I don't think he knows what he's seeing right now besides things close up."

Ben's eyes flared with desire as he gazed at Jessie's breasts. Blushing she firmed her lips and said, "Maybe a walk would do you good. You seem to have too much energy to sit around the house."

"Maybe I'll just go and see what Morgan's up to then." As he headed to go out the kitchen door both women simultaneously said, "I'll go with you."

The three adults all formed a semi-circle behind Nathan as he bent to look into the lens and told Morgan to hold for just a moment. The new photography equipment was much faster than the older tin type style and the people didn't need to retain a stoic manner for several minutes. These new photos would be made from a negative and could be used over and over, even able to send a copy to a newspaper hundreds of miles away.

Ben was sincerely interested in the equipment and how the light worked with the lens. He talked with his brother about the new horses being brought in at the end of the week and when Morgan planned on going back to Washington D. C. or Austin. Jessie and Mary stayed quiet, watching Nathan, but out of the sides of their eyes watching Morgan as he moved and sat as Nathan instructed him.

Finally, with one last look and raised eye brows at Mary, Jessie took a yawning William into the house for his nap leaving the rest of the adults outside.

CHAPTER TWELVE

Knowing Morgan was busy with Ben after dinner, Mary peered into the empty tipi, empty of inhabitants anyway. The smell of the hides and buffalo robes mingled with the wood smoke and tobacco. It took her back years, to the time when such a tipi was her home, where she lived every day and slept every night. She walked across to touch the feathered head dress hanging from one of the poles, another held the carved-out bison head, the pointed horns shiny against the mat of fur worn by a warrior during battles.

She picked up a wire of shells and pieces of horn, making a clacking sound as they hit together as they would when worn by a brave through the piercing in his ears. Morgan didn't wear his unless he was in Comanche dress, the same with his hair. He dressed English when in the ranch house or the few times she saw him return from Austin. She rubbed the smooth wood of the center pole that held the flap open to let the fire's smoke out. It seemed a little surreal that once this was her home, or rather a tipi just like it. A few personal items making it Morgan's rather than any other tribal member's home.

Mary realized she had been snooping in Morgan's tipi long enough and turned to go, finding her gaze captivated by the man standing in the entrance now closed behind him. Mary's hand went instinctively to her hip where her knife had hung for her whole life until the Burgess adopted her.

"Here, take mine," Morgan said as he threw the knife from the waist of his breechcloth so it buried itself to the hilt into the sand a few feet from her.

Mary relaxed and tried to smile, but couldn't come up with one so said quietly, "I'm sorry for intruding. I was curious as to whether I could enter a tipi and not break down."

"You seem to be able to hold your own quite well. Is there anything else you would like to test yourself with?" he asked, his voice deep and low, just between the two of them.

"I, ah, no. I think I should be leaving," she said, realizing she would have to go around the large man in order to escape.

"Are you sure? I've noticed you've been watching me closely. I'm willing to allow you to get a firsthand experience," he said, teasing her as she felt herself blush.

"I was drawing you. Jessie wanted me to get all the family members," Mary said, holding her head up and meeting his dark gaze evenly.

"I'm flattered and am still offering myself for your further study. Does my body not interest you?" He stepped so he was now right in front of her without touching.

Mary dropped her gaze to his broad chest marked with scars of success and loss, scars earned by tribal trials and enemy weapons. She raised her hand slowly without looking at his face and drew her finger lightly over the horizontal scars caused when he became a warrior. Then she moved them over a mark where a spear had barely missed his heart. She drew her brows down in concern and finally spoke.

"You have fought many battles, but most of your wounds were given to you by your own tribe. How do you reconcile your life as a Comanche and as a man in a suit?" she asked, finally able to meet his challenge.

Morgan had been standing there with his eyes closed, but opened them to answer her question. "It is because I have a foot in both worlds. I have a loyalty and respect for the family who trained and taught me how to live and I have loyalty and love for the family who let me be what I wanted to be, allowed me to follow an unusual path, yet still welcome me home," he told her, allowing her to continue to touch his body.

"It's not the same with me. I only wanted to go back to the Apache village and my family, but I think I always knew they had been killed the day I was taken captive. I had no other place to call home," she said, letting her hand drop to her side.

"What is your name?" Morgan asked simply.

"You know my name," she said as Morgan shook his head slowly and she admitted, "My name. I was called, Mourning Dove. My mother thought I looked like a small bird bundled on the cradle board."

Morgan tasted the name on his lips. "Mourning Dove, I like that. It suits you - quiet, watchful."

Mary smiled, adding in self-deprecation, "Grey and unassuming. Just one of many, not interesting or notable."

"I find you interesting and notable, Mourning Dove. I think you have spent so much of your life so no one would notice you, you think that is who you are. I see a much different woman in front of me," he told her, placing his hands on her slender waist, letting them lightly caress her shape.

Dropping her head, Mary got quiet. "I wasn't like most captives. I wasn't used by the braves, not after the first day or two. After that I was treated as the chief's niece because his sister wanted me to replace her daughter who had drowned. I'm not what you think I am."

"I think you're a beautiful young woman who I have found very attractive from the first time I saw you and you tried to stab me with a butter knife."

At that, she raised her head and said fiercely, "It was a bread knife and it was sharp. It was the only thing I had close at hand."

"And I thought you so brave to try to protect William and Jessie from me, even though if I were there to do harm, I could have gotten past you soon enough," he said truthfully.

"I only thought to buy Jessie some time to get outside and call to the men in the stable. I knew I wasn't a match against you. Who would be?" she said as she sized him up again.

"Be careful with your eyes, they are like a razor when you're angry and I haven't done anything for you to be frightened or angry at me about. Or is it that I am what I am?" he asked her, seemingly hoping to get an answer he could live with.

Mary gazed into his eyes again saying, "I don't know. I'm attracted to you, your strength, your intelligence, even your living in two worlds. I am afraid of what that could mean to me. What your plans are for me, for I feel you have some, but I am afraid of them."

"That's fair, I'm not sure myself. I never thought I could bring a woman into this life, my life in two worlds, but you seem to already be doing so yourself, just not as

181

dramatically anymore. You have taken your separate worlds and conquered them one at a time. Is the Whiteman's world the one you feel the most comfortable in?"

"No, but I was not given much of a choice. I like wearing the White woman's clothing at times, the pretty hats and jewelry, but I am most comfortable in buckskins and moccasins with my hair hanging in braids."

"I'd like to see you in nothing at all," Morgan said as he bent his head and covered her mouth with his, allowing his tongue to enter her mouth and move freely within her.

Mary raised herself up to get closer to him as he let his hand slide down her hip and rest lower, his thumb strumming against her softness. Morgan lowered them to the bison skin and lay down facing her, stroking up her body, taking the dress with it, leaving it at her waist so his hand could feel the contours of her hip and legs.

She returned the kisses as best as she could. A kiss wasn't something she was familiar with, but she had seen Emily and the Major as well as Ben and Jessie kiss when they greeted each other or when they were parting. This meeting of the mouths was something more intimate, nothing Mary was familiar with.

Unbuttoning the front of the blue gingham dress, Morgan moved his hand to cover her breast as the nipple hardened in his palm before moving to the other, covering the first with moist lips. Mary twisted to allow him more access, but didn't know how to control the feelings that were building inside her. How to let Morgan know she liked what he was doing when he took the mystery from her.

"Mourning Dove, I think we better slow down or stop or we may go beyond what is acceptable in polite society," he said as he continued to kiss her lips and press his hand over her now damp breast.

"So what world are we in now? Not the Comanche or I would have been under you by now, so is it the Whiteman's?" she asked, not understanding what was truly going on between them. She was used to the male taking what he wanted and the female being subservient.

"This is our world. We do what we want here. I want you very much, but I don't make the rules here, you do," he told her surprisingly.

"Then I want to continue. I like what we're doing, but can I touch you? Is that part of it?" she asked innocently.

"Certainly, and I'll continue to touch you." He returned to kissing her after removing the top portion of the dress and the camisole beneath it exposing her to him and his lips.

Mary was enjoying the feel of his muscles as they bunched and stretched under her small fluttering hands. When she followed the line of his body down over his hip and her hands stroked his thigh, Morgan became more amorous and pushed Mary flat with her back to the ground and lay his weight on top of her.

Immediately Mary began thrashing and pushing and making little gasping sounds as she tried to free herself of his weight, of his dominance. "No, no, get off, me. I want to go, I don't want this," she said as she pushed at the surprised Morgan.

"Shhh, Mourning Dove, I wasn't trying to hurt you. If you don't want to make love we won't, just don't be so upset. I didn't understand the limits," he said as he tried to pull her back down next to him, his long body more at ease than he had been before.

Mary regretted what now seemed to be her over reaction, "I don't know how to handle this. I was very afraid of you for a time. I'm sorry, I don't know what to do."

"You were doing everything just fine. Do you want to go back into the house or do you want to stay and make love? I will be very careful not to frighten you, I promise, but if this isn't what you want, you should leave me now," he told her honestly, knowing he would let her go.

"I like what we're doing. I really like you and how you feel and how you make me feel," she said, not knowing what else to do, not wanting to leave him either.

"Then let's try this." Removing the loin cloth leaving him with only the tight sash around his waist, he lifted her over to straddle him, letting her warm female part nestle his engorged male part.

She knew her eyes widened and her smile even wider as she moved above him, letting him slide through her warm moist lower folds. Morgan groaned and placed his hands on her hips to help her slide across him before placing them up to cup both breasts. Mary rose a little and let the now slick penis slip into her channel and Morgan made another groan of pleasure deep down inside his throat.

"This is how it should always be for us, Mourning Dove. We fit together so well. Do you feel that way, too?" he asked as he let her control their mounting passion.

"I like what we're doing. It's not like anything I've felt before. I can't believe this is part of who we are, it makes more sense to me now. I understand much more."

As she increased speed, she felt little muscles tighten and spasm and she collapsed in utter bliss on to Morgan's chest as he pulled her to him. Raising his hips to reach deeply inside her, he culminated in his climax.

"Oh, Morgan, I didn't know how wonderful this is. I can't thank you enough for showing me," she said, smiling as she listened to his heart regain its normal beat.

"I should thank you. It's the polite thing to do, I'm sure, since you were in control," he said, laughing at being thanked for making love. "I only remained in position and enjoyed every moment of it. Now lay down here and let me cover you, it seems to have gotten chilly." Wrapping her in a blanket, he curved his body around her in a protective cocoon.

Morgan forced himself to stay awake until he heard Mary's even breathing. He held her tightly, worrying about what she would do in the light of day. Would all this seem alien and foreign to her or would she understand he wanted them to be together, as a couple. Could she continue to live in two worlds?

His world of the Comanche would constantly remind her of the years of captivity and of the killing of her family. Could what he offer her, replace all that she had lost? All that she had endured? And if she couldn't live with him as a wife of a Comanche chief, could she live with him as the wife to a political lobbyist in Austin or Washington D. C.? His worlds were varied and often collided, but so had hers it would seem. Were they strong enough together to live as one when they both had trouble living as two?

A few hours later Morgan woke Mary from a sound sleep, originally to say she should go into the house before anyone was awake, but other ideas came to mind and he found her responding to his initial hip thrusts. He placed one hand over a breast and the other on the mound between her legs then slid his finger into the welcoming warmth. Mary showed her appreciation by rocking with him and he entered her from behind, kissing and sucking on her neck and shoulder. Mary pushed back to him and began the throes of an orgasm that sent her into stronger reactions than she had earlier that evening. Morgan finished simultaneously, crushing her to him, as he tried not to hurt her with the strength of his passion.

"Are you all right? I didn't mean to hold you so tightly, I don't want to frighten you again," he whispered into her ear as they both recovered.

"I don't think I could be afraid of you, Morgan. I trust you completely not to hurt me now."

Morgan felt humbled, knowing even after what she had been through, she trusted him not to harm her. He wondered if he could be trusted or if they were enjoying a moment out of time to be together as just a man and woman, not a Numunuu and an Apache captive. Morgan never thought of her as such, but the truth of the matter was that if Mary had never been taken captive, he wouldn't have her in his arms right now. As an Apache, he would never have been let near her, her family would never have condoned the relationship.

"Mourning Dove, you have to go inside before anyone wakes up. I hate to let you go, but there will be all hell to pay if we are found together like this," he said, kissing the side of her mouth and cheeks and eyes, making a map of her face for him to dream of when he was alone.

"I will see you later today then. I must find my

clothes." She dressed in the semi darkness, the early dawn beginning to show over the horizon.

Mary had just closed the door when a voice in the shadows stated, "A little early for a walk isn't it, Mary." Jessie was heating water for an early morning tea before William woke for his feeding.

Stiffening with surprise, Mary, realizing who spoke relaxed and answered, "Too much coffee with dinner last night, I guess. Mother Nature called." Then she hurried across the kitchen to the doorway to escape upstairs.

Glancing down at her light robe over her night gown and her bare feet, Jessie grabbed the door handle with force as she tried to keep her temper under control. She said crisply at the closed tipi flap, "Morgan, I need to speak with you."

"Come in, Little Sister, I wasn't expecting you," Morgan's deep voice answered, still sounding sleepy.

Yanking back the skin covering the opening, she entered the tipi. "Morgan, I expected better of you. Your mother would be disappointed if she were to hear of this. Mary was under her protection after all," Jessie, her hands on her hips, stood over her brother-in-law.

"I apologize for not standing in the presence of a lady, but...." And he waved over the blanket to explain his lack of attire.

"It's not me you have to apologize to. Mary is your family's guest, compromised by being a captive once. Now she finally has a chance of a new kind of life. I don't understand how you let this happen," she said, disappointment evident in her face and voice.

"I'm not sure either. It wasn't my intent. I mean, I always thought I would never marry or have children or live a life simply for what I wanted. I had dedicated my life to finding the new life for my people, help them become comfortable in life as they will have to live it," he said, sitting up, but making sure not to embarrass her with his nudity.

Kneeling on the buffalo rugs she said, "Marry or have children, you said. Are you thinking Mary could be the woman to change your mind about living alone? Could you see her as part of your life from now on?" Realizing Morgan may have actual feelings toward Mary made Jessie rethink her original chastisement.

"Mourning Dove, her name is Mourning Dove and I don't think she's comfortable with the Whiteman's world, but she thinks that is the only choice she has. I don't want her to stay with me because she has no other way to live, because she lost the life she was meant to have. I want her to choose me and my life," he confessed.

"I agree the Burgess are not a true family for Mary, I mean, Mourning Dove, but that will need to be her decision. I actually hoped she and Nathan would find a connection through their art. He deserves a kind sweet wife. But I can see the bond between you and she could be even stronger, although there are more hurdles to get over," she said, letting her memory go back to times Mourning Dove and Nathan had been together under the canvas shade.

"So, you won't be ripping me apart over the dinner table?" he asked smiling.

"Not yet, but that will depend on whether or not Mourning Dove is hurt by you or anything you've done to her. It only took one time for me to get William. I hope you were sensible last night," she admonished.

Morgan closed his eyes, evidently realizing he hadn't thought about protecting Mourning Dove. At the contrite expression on his face as he finally opened his eyes, Jessie stood up saying, "This better not turn out the same way for you two. It becomes a wall between the two people involved and a burden to everyone else."

"Have I ever told you how right for my brother you are?"

Shaking her head at his attempt to sweet talk her, she turned and went out to the brightening sky.

When Jessie entered the kitchen, she jumped at the raspy voice of her husband as he leaned against the cupboard. "You've been gone a long time. I came to find you." The expression he gave her as he stood there wearing only his trousers, the buttons open at the waist was unreadable.

"I wanted to speak privately with Morgan, this is the only time we could be undisturbed," she told her husband, still unable to read his mood or emotions.

"Did you get everything all talked out then?" he asked in that same quiet, monotone voice.

"Yes, is William awake?" she asked, trying to change the subject.

"He was beginning to fuss and suck his hand so I came down here to find you. Do you still want this tea you began to make?" he asked, turning away from her.

"No, I'll go up to the baby before he wakes the whole house. Once he thinks he's been forgotten he never calms down and ends up spitting up half of what he's eaten."

She hurried through the doorway while Ben stared out the window at the tipi, trying to decide to follow his

189

wife up to bed or go out and punch his brother in the face. He had been unable to keep looking at the innocence in her eyes when they had been speaking, but he knew she lied to him.

Was there something he missed between Morgan and his wife? Was his brother more the man Jessie wanted being so different from her in so many ways yet alike in others? They both empathized with people whose lives were being destroyed by outside forces. They both dedicated their lives to helping those less fortunate while keeping a way of life from ending. They both were strong, emotionally strong, thinkers who put their ideas into practice. Neither sat on the sideline letting others do what needed to be done.

Rather than go and beat the hell out of his brother, he decided to go to his family, his only chance to keep Jessie with him was to bind her to him with William. Showing her their family was what truly mattered.

CHAPTER THIRTEEN

The interviews began to spread to a few other bands of Comanche and Morgan was right there to insure nothing dangerous occurred. The tipis and clothing and utensils were pretty much identical, but Nathan found some interesting faces and he and Mary spent their time together photographing and sketching sometimes side by side.

The unusual group with Morgan received a lot of interest from the Numunuu having been closed off to the rest of the world for so long. They asked as many questions of Ben as Ben could get answers from them. The Numunuu's curiosity driven by the openness the group had shown towards the Numunuu.

Jessie had learned to bring gifts of dried beans or rice to these groups further from towns and the women were interested in William and his diapers since a Comanche child his age would still be bundled in a cradle board with moss as a diaper. They touched his white, white skin and smiled as he seemed to smile at them.

Morgan was more relaxed now, finding his people were being on their best behavior with his family. He renewed old acquaintances which helped Jessie find new stories of the tribes' history while Ben did the necessary interpretation. Explaining to Jessie he would write down the more graphic descriptions for her to incorporate into her writings later.

Mary still cared for William for most of the day, allowing Jessie to speak to the elders unencumbered and without anything to distract her. Ben and Jessie were walking back to the canvas shade when Jessie's brows creased in concern as she searched around.

Nathan was taking photos of the horses being cared for and painted with red hand prints as if going out on a raiding party, but there was no sign of Mary or William watching him.

"Ben, I don't see the baby or Mary and the cradle is empty, even the blanket he sleeps on is gone," she said worriedly, searching for any sign Mary left a note or message as to where she had taken the baby.

The sketch pad was opened as usual and a group of four men were drawn there, their faces and top half of their bodies complete. There were only rough lines to catch the men's stances and proportionate size to one another.

Coming out of a near-by tipi, Morgan must have noticed the frantic expressions on his brother and sister-in-law's faces. "What's happened?" He peered around asking, "Where's Mourning Dove? She told me she was staying here with William while he napped."

"Neither of them was here when we got back, even his blanket is gone. It's too hot to wrap him in a blanket, Mary knows that. He'll get a heat rash," Jessie said, still trying to understand why Mary took William out from the shade in the middle of the afternoon.

Nathan returned then, but didn't have any idea where Mary might have gone and peered around. "What's different now than when we got here?"

Morgan asked if she was in one of the nearby tipis, but most of those had the bottoms rolled up to catch any breeze. No sign of Mary's gingham dress showed anywhere.

Nathan continued, "There was something else over there...men. I know, I was going to photograph them, but Mary said they weren't Comanche. She said one was Apache, one a Kiowa and the two others *mestizaje*, mixed blood. All were wearing military hats with gold braid, buckskin leggings and loin cloths. Two wore long sleeve shirts and the other two Calvary shirts. All of them wore a leather boot of some sort."

"Are these the men?" asked Ben as he showed Nathan the half-finished sketch.

"Yes, they were right over there," he said, pointing to a now empty site.

Returning from talking to some of the tribe members, Morgan was in time to see the sketch held up for Nathan. "What were they doing here? Two of those men your father had banned from the Rangers for being too vicious with the prisoners and raping the female captives. The other two I don't know, but if they're hanging around together, they may be of the same mind."

Jessie grasped her husband's shirt. "Oh, Ben, why would they take our baby? You don't think they'd hurt him, do you?" She was trying to hear anyone tell her that William was all right. That the men wouldn't harm an infant. All the stories to the contrary she tried to push to the back of her mind. She would not think the unthinkable. She would not allow herself to give up hope both would be found.

Morgan turned away coming back moments later. "No one saw all of them leave together, but they're gone and so are all their horses. I have to think they took Mary and William. I have friends who are going with me to track them."

Ben said, grabbing his rifle, "I'm going, too. Nathan do you have a gun just in case?" At Nathan's nod he told Jessie, "Don't worry, I'll get them both back."

A group of four braves, most carrying bows and arrows and one a long-barreled rifle brought Morgan's horse up and Morgan mounted telling his brother, "Then you better put on a loin cloth because we are going in disguised as a hunting party to lessen their suspicions. You will have to blend in with us and ride in the middle."

One of the youngest braves jumped off his pony and handed the reins to a friend as he ran towards a nearby tipi. He returned with a loin cloth that an already half naked Ben accepted as he kicked off his trousers from his bare feet and tied the familiar garment around his waist, his less than tan legs and buttocks showing in the sun light.

Another Comanche pony was brought for Ben and the group rode off, having found the trail of the four men. The other men hadn't bothered to cover up their horses' shoe prints when they left the village.

Jessie and Nathan were going to follow. Jessie didn't want to wait until Ben brought William back to her. She wanted to be as close as possible when he was rescued and, she feared, Mary would need a female friend, also.

Nathan borrowed two more horses and took extra bullets from his equipment box. "Do you think you can still keep up? I know you haven't been riding astride since the baby," he said, making sure Jessie was ready for the rigorous ride.

"I can do anything to get to my son and Mary. Let's get going. I know we want to stay back, but I don't want to lose them completely," she said, pulling herself up onto the blanket, glad she had continued to wear the split leather skirt every day to the encampments.

Nathan led since he was the better of the two of them for reading tracks and as they got out to the windblown desert area, the ground became hard and more difficult to follow a trail.

Morgan was down on the ground, fingering the bright piece of cloth snagged on a sage bush. "Is this something Mary would wear? Does it seem familiar?"

Ben took it from him saying, "It's a piece of William's blanket, it's looks like it's been ripped from the hem." He stared into the horizon in a chance they would see the group of riders.

One of the other braves called to them. He had circled outward trying to find a sign of the other horses when he saw another bright piece of fabric stabbed by a cactus.

"It must be Mourning Dove. She is leaving us pieces of fabric so we can follow her," Morgan said, leaping back onto his pony.

The band of braves took off in the direction indicated by the wind and the fabric, hoping the other four men weren't travelling as fast, one of their horses carrying the extra weight of Mary. Possibly even taking rest periods along the way.

The braves had to concede to the heat and allow their horses a resting time, keeping them moving, but at a much less break-neck pace. The only thing that kept Ben from howling out his frustration was the fact the other group of riders were probably having to do the same thing. They came upon a site that appeared to have been used as a resting spot, a wad of material hidden slightly under a rock and part of a cactus broken off, the kind that stung long after the initial prick to the skin.

Mounting his horse, Ben and the hunting band began following their prey once again. A couple of more hours and they saw the group they had been tracking sitting and standing in the horizon. The rescuing braves decided to ride up to them as a hunting party as they had planned. Nothing should have made the four men concerned about being followed by the Comanche since they hadn't taken anything belonging to the Comanche.

Ben had to remain hidden till they could take the men by surprise so Morgan kept to his horse as Ben held on to the Comanche style saddle. Hanging down at the side of the pony, a familiar trick the two brothers practiced as boys whenever they were bored. It was one the Comanche used, hiding behind their horse right into the thick of things. White men didn't shoot rider-less horses, considered just a waste of bullets. But such a trick had cost unwary men more than a bullet.

The horse Ben had been riding was being pulled alongside one of the brave's. They didn't want to go in shooting since no one could see Mary or the baby. Ben would end up behind the kidnappers while the rest of the braves made noise and rode as if they were going to ride right into the four men.

At Morgan's nod he began whooping and riding toward the group still on foot and the four men began shooting at him. Morgan fell to the ground and lay there as if dead. Ben hoped none of the bullets actually hit his brother, but he couldn't check. It was more important to get behind the group of men and surprise them. Then he could get both Mary and the baby out of harm's way and the braves could finish them off if that's what they wanted. Ben realized the thought was as blood-thirsty as any the Comanche had but didn't care. Saving Mary and William was the most important thing, right now. His hatred for the men who endangered them would be satisfied later, either by an arrow of the braves or a rope of the Whiteman.

As planned, the four men ignored the rider-less horse, their focus on the constantly moving Comanche braves. Ben dropped from the horse as soon as he saw he was behind the men. Grabbing his knife, he put it to the neck of the first man he came to slicing ruthlessly. He saw one of the other men turn to shoot at him and he placed the now dead man he held around the neck toward his comrade and he took the bullet meant for Ben. Grabbing the end of the still hot rifle, he yanked hard, tugging the man holding it off balance, allowing Ben to make a slicing movement and that man dropped in a pool of blood, too.

Mary was crouched over a crying baby, but appeared to be safe and unhurt so Ben took his attention to the next man a little way away who was still unaware of the silent deaths of his two accomplices. The other braves were coming closer and closer to the last two men and an arrow entered the farthest man's chest, making him give an odd grimace and drop his rifle as he tried to pull the arrow out. He died with the arrow clutched in his hands. The last man felt Ben's knife against his throat just as remounted Morgan was going to jump from his speeding horse onto him.

The man struggled and Ben pushed the knife home, glad William was too young to remember this day and the blood and the men killed for daring to touch him. Ben turned to see Morgan gently lift Mary and cradle her and the baby, whispering something into her ears, for her to hear only.

The rest of the braves whooped war cries they hadn't been able to use in battle in their life time. Their ponies pranced and rifle shots were sent into the air in celebration. Soon it was quiet again as they dismounted and rifled through the dead men's belongings, the spoils of war to the victors. Neither Morgan nor Ben wanted to reprimand them. This had always been how wealth was accumulated, the men's horses would belong to the braves, also, as soon as they were used to take the dead men in to the fort.

Ben held his son, trying to sooth him knowing only Jessie was going to be able to settle him after such an experience. But his son's heartfelt cries were music to his ears.

Mary hadn't been crying as Morgan had thought. She had been wrapped around William to protect him from flying bullets and arrows. All she knew was what the four trackers had said. There was a Comanche war party attacking and they were all going to be killed or tortured.

"I wanted to save William., I couldn't let them take him. I had put cactus pieces under the horse blankets. They began to act up and refused to let anyone on them again so the guides stopped to find out what had happened. I thought I could slow things down if we had to walk, time to get found, but I never thought a band of

Comanche would come to my rescue," she told Morgan as he turned her from the eyes of the others.

"I would never let anyone take you without following them to the edge of hell and then push them in. These men thought they were going to get back at the Major, little did they know the hornets' nest they struck. My brother is more Numunuu then he knows. When he joined my tribe, our blood flowed together, he is me and I am him. You did good today leaving the trail of cloth, Mourning Dove, but why did they take you? To keep you from sounding the alarm?"

"No, I told them I was William's wet nurse and he would die without me so they took me, too. None of them wanted to care for a baby. They were going to ask for a huge ransom from the Major, something about him owing them," she spoke quickly, emotion making her excited. She looked at Morgan as she began to realize how much danger she had been in. "I wasn't needed as a hostage, was I? No one was going to pay to get an Apache returned to them. I was expendable."

As if reading her mind, he said, "I would have paid anything for your return to me. I have never been so afraid since William's birth and that was for the pain his death would have caused Ben." He whispered to her ear, trying to make her understand how very dear she was to him. "You are more precious than a part of my heart, of more value to me than my own life."

When she tried to touch his face, Mourning Dove flinched at the pain in her hands. "I had to grab the cactus with both hands to break pieces off the tough plant. When I told the men I had to have some privacy to relieve myself, I placed them under the horses' blankets." Morgan took her hands in his and kissed them, uncaring if the other braves saw him.

"Can we tear some more of that blanket to wrap your hands?" he asked, his brows drawn down in concern.

"My petticoat, I can rip a strip off of that." As soon as she said it, Morgan lifted her skirt and tore the top ruffle off then began to gently wrap her hands, knowing she had been in a lot of pain without complaining.

Ben stood up with the still whimpering William saying, "Two riders coming from the same direction as us." As everyone watched, Ben said, "It's Jessie and Nathan. She probably wouldn't stay once we left. I should have tied her up for him."

Mary, getting more comfortable with her rescuers said, "She would have talked Nathan or someone into letting her lose, nothing was going to keep her from William. I knew that so I tried to slow them down whenever I could. I knew Jessie would be back to feed William soon after they took us."

The braves were getting anxious to get back to the village to show off their plunder, pearl handled hand guns and Remington rifles along with coins and knives. Morgan told them to go ahead, that they would keep the men's horses for a while, but he would make sure they got them when they were no longer needed.

Jessie reached her husband and almost fell off her horse, she was so anxious and worried about her son. Ben caught her, helping her sit as he placed the still upset William in her arms. The baby quieted immediately, nuzzling his mother, but not demanding the feeding he had been denied earlier.

Jessie wiped the tears from her face and kept murmuring to her son, her husband wrapping his arm around her. "Is Mary alright? I saw her with Morgan and she seemed almost too calm, we need to watch her for shock. I know we owe her for protecting William."

Nathan saw the couples taking care of each other and said, "I'll check on the horses, maybe get these bodies tied onto their saddles. I take it we are going to have to take them in with us?"

Mary called out in a clear voice, "Check under the two paint's blankets and remove the cactus. I hate to hurt an animal, but I had to slow our progress. Once it became dark you wouldn't have seen my trail I was leaving. You could have lost us in the hills."

"I'll try to make a pad if the hides are broken, but horses have pretty tough skin," Morgan said, and smiled as she lifted her skirt once more and tore more of her petticoat off.

"There's not much more left of this, you know," Morgan teased, "You'll be wearing less than Ben any minute."

"How did you get him to wear, well, what he's wearing?" she asked.

"We were going to come in as a hunting party if we had to, catch them unawares, when they weren't expecting an ambush," Morgan told her. "Ben would have stood out and we weren't sure the men hadn't known what he looked like so they would panic. Maybe hurt you or William if we simply rode up."

"I think they may have known him, but they were not aware of your connection. I never heard them say your name at all."

"No one, but my family and work associates call me Morgan, I'm Toshawi, White Knife due to my mixed blood."

"I know, I was told when you came to my village and talked with the chief and other elders. I remember when you rode in and when you rode out," she told him, letting him know the time he failed to rescue her.

He held her to his chest and said, "I'm sorry. Back then I wasn't in a position to save the captives, but if I had seen you, I would have come back for you."

"I understand, I do, and my mother would not let me leave the tipi that whole day since she was afraid her brother would give me to you as a present if you showed any interest."

"I never accepted captives as presents or to use them while I was staying with a tribe. I found polite ways to turn them down without offending the giver and if I found one in my tipi for the night, I left her to herself saying I had an injury that prevented my participation in any kind of copulation."

"You don't need to tell me these things, Morgan. I don't have the right to question your life or your choices. We each had to make our way as best we could, it's just easier for a male," she told him honestly.

"I want to have a very honest conversation with you, but now is not the time. I think the horses have had enough of a rest. I should be helping Nathan with those bodies, if we're to get home before dark."

Jessie called Mary over to sit with her when the men went to load the horses and get ready to make the return trip. William was suckling lustily, happy to have his mother near him again and Jessie had already made a promise he was literally never going to be out of her sight.

"I want to thank you for taking care of William. I know facing what was basically captivity again wasn't an easy decision. I won't forget your helping me, I owe you anything you want. I know a little of what happened between you and Morgan, but if you need me to intervene or help you get home or start over somewhere, I'll make it happen."

"I understand, and there isn't anything between Morgan and me, not enough anyway. He has chosen a life for himself and I need to find a life for me. I hope it includes a husband and children, but I'm not sure where that leaves me. I need to find another displaced male Apache who wants to marry a Comanche captive Christian woman who is known as Mary Burgess." Jessie knew the old Mary was back and ready to roar.

It was a tired group who found themselves coming up to the ranch house, the Major and Emily coming out to meet them, not knowing what had them home so late. Ben told his father he would talk with him later, but the four bodies on the back of the horses needed to be taken to the fort in the morning.

"Go inside, sons, I'll take care of the bodies and the horses. Are these yours Morgan or do they need to be taken back?" he asked, seeing the strange ponies along with Morgan's usual mount.

"The horses the dead men are on and those others all go back to the Tenewa tribe, I told them I would deliver them personally. I'll go with you to the fort and tell them what happened, Ben will need to come, too, since he killed most of them."

The Major looked at his youngest son with concern, taking in his dress as a Comanche brave which wasn't normal for Ben.

"I need to get Jessie settled, it's a long story and we'll need to eat and get some rest," he told the older man and then turned to follow his wife and child into the kitchen.

The Major pushed Morgan toward the house with the others. Then took the horses' reins along with one of the stable hands who had come out from the bunkhouse when the group rode in.

CHAPTER FOURTEEN

Emily rose from the big table in the dining room having had breakfast as a family there earlier. The Major, Ben and Morgan had just left to take the trip to the fort. They were hoping to get home that evening if they didn't need to go before the judge. They packed in case they had to stay the night and Emily sent food to eat on the way.

Jessie turned to Nathan, the only one left with her at the table and said, "I want to thank you once again for getting me to William yesterday. I appreciate your always coming to my rescue, like in the Himalayas."

"Just call and I'll be there, Jessie. I owe you and your father a great deal. Without your recommendations and support of my work, I would still be in some small southern town taking photographs of the newly freedmen and their families."

"Never, your talent would have shown through and someone else would have taken you in and dragged you to the back of beyond to take photos of long dead dinosaur bones or the snowy peaks in Nepal," She teased then said, "You're sure you need to leave today? I would love for you to stay longer. I promise it won't be as exciting as yesterday."

"Jessie, *ma Cherie*, you cannot promise any such thing nor would I want you to. I would almost worry if something like yesterday didn't occur whenever I am with you. I am so glad it ended well, for us at least." He smiled then added, "I like your family, Jessie. It is exactly the type of family I would have envisioned for you. Just not normal, that would have been too boring for you."

"I wasn't planning on a family at all, Nathan. It has thrown off all my plans," she admitted.

"Plans are made to be flexible, *ma Cherie*, is that not what your father told us? You have plans and then there are The Plans. You were the premise of The Plans. He made his plans to study here or there, but you were the center of his real-life plans. He would be so happy to know you found a man who understood you, allowed you to study on your honeymoon, is allowing you and actually accompanying you while you study the Comanche, a tribe he has a bad history with. No, you are very lucky in your choice of husband and your son will bring you more joy than you can ever imagine."

"I know. I'm a very selfish person and Ben deserves so much more. I do agree with you about William, but am I so selfish, like my parents were, to deny my son siblings? Family who will be with him, help him when Ben and I die? Or will he be so involved in some study he actually forgets the anniversary of my passing?" she confessed to one of her only friends.

"Ahh, *ma Cherie*, are you sure you are too busy to remember or have you buried yourself into this work so you don't need to face your memories? I miss your father, also, but he would want you to live as well as study. He never expected you to live his life, after all he had your mother with him for over fifteen years before she died. It wasn't until her death that he began to really take you seriously as a student of anthropology. You tried to fill her shoes in a way, to help your father continue working in his chosen field. But make sure this is your real love and not a reflection of your father. I don't want to find you threw away real life, a real family simply to study lives that are dying or have died out."

"I've thought about that, too. The part about living my life rather than studying someone else's to see where they ended up. I think I need to find a way to merge my life and my studies. And I want to visit you and meddle with your life, too. I'm sure there is a woman somewhere who is getting tired of waiting for you," she teased and stood to take William out of the cradle and carry him with her upstairs.

There was a light knock on the door and Jessie let Mary in as she quickly closed the door behind her, talking so quietly Jessie had trouble hearing her at first. "You said you would do anything for me. Were you serious?"

Jessie said worriedly, "Yes, of course. What's wrong?"

"I want Nathan to take me with him." As Jessie's eyebrows rose in surprise, Mary went on, "I want to leave before Morgan returns and talks me out of it. I don't have any strength to go against his wishes, he makes me so mixed up when we're together. I'm not returning to my adoptive family. I think I've out grown them, too. But this will be best for me."

"Are you sure? I think Morgan has strong feelings for you. Are you set on leaving?" At Mary's slow nod, Jessie continued, "I have money and if you're going to start out somewhere else, I have some dresses and shoes you can take since we're close to the same size or at least we were before the baby. Let me help you pack since Nathan wants to leave soon so he can catch the stage out of town."

Nathan helped Mary get her stage ticket and made sure her bags along with his equipment were packed on the coach when it arrived. He was dressed better than most of the other men while Mary wore a summer weight dress with flared cape and a little hat with veil and bows on top of her braided crown. Nathan's glare kept the mouths of the other three men riding inside the coach shut and when they reached a town that had a railroad, they left the stage together.

"Are you sure this is where you want to be? Isn't this your home town, where your adopted family lives?" Nathan asked as they waited for his train.

"I feel more comfortable here, but I probably won't stay long. I think I will join a missionary group and work at one of the missions teaching English. After working with Jessie, I realize the tribes will need to speak multiple languages to survive, but English can't be the only language or the culture will be lost. I'm only one person, but possibly I can help," she told him as they heard the train get closer to the station.

"It has been a pleasure to have worked with you and I wish you the best, Mourning Dove. I hope you find what you're searching for." He tipped his hat and placed his bags with the porter who had stepped down from the train.

Waving until the train pulled out, Mary turned to face the town that would be home again for at least a few weeks. She hadn't let the Reverend or his family know she was returning because she had made the decision on the spur of the moment. She had to acknowledge she really didn't have plans or know of any missions that wanted another teacher. Jessie was more than generous with her payment for the drawings, although Mary considered most of it a loan that she would pay back.

Having made arrangements for her larger case to be held at the station, she took the smaller satchel and walked toward a boarding house she knew catered to single women and widows. Mrs. Brown, a widow and owner, knew the Reverend and Mary was hoping that would ensure her a room.

Facing the usually complaining business woman, Mary kept a tight smile pasted on her face. "I understand the Reverend's house is probably over crowded. They will keep taking in all these unwanted children." Then the over-weight woman seemed to have realized to whom she was speaking and patted her hair saying patronizingly, "I know my Christian duty so I can let you have the small room off the kitchen usually set aside for the cook and maid. If you will agree to help in the kitchen and maybe laundry, I can discount the room. Of course, you would have to enter and leave by the back door."

Mary explained in her best adopted daughter voice, "Of course, helping with the meals would give me something to do with my time during the day. I probably won't be here long, only until a missionary group forms to go to one of the reservations."

"Good. I've set out some pork chops for tonight and you can figure out what else you want to make to go with them. I usually have a soup, too, and four sides plus desert. Everything is in the pantry." The proprietress of the boarding house stood up and brushed down her dress, dismissing Mary so she could go and begin her chores.

Carrying her bag to the room off the kitchen, she noted the bare minimum of furniture and single oil lamp, thinking it was probably more than she was going to have once she joined a missionary group. She might send Jessie's dresses back to her since they would be out of place in Mary's new world.

Evidently gossip in the town was as good as Mary remembered. A couple of days after moving into the boarding house her adopted mother, Mrs. Burgess, came to call. "Mother, how nice to see you. I was going to send a note around, but I've been so busy since getting back," Mary explained, taking off her apron and sitting down in one of the chairs opposite Mrs. Burgess on the sofa.

"You appear very well, Mary, I am pleased. Mrs. Edwards wrote and said how helpful you were with her daughter-in-law's work. The woman actually gets published internationally and has exhibits in the Smithsonian Museum in the Capital. Your name might be right next to hers when she finishes this new report." Searching Mary's face as if unable to believe such things about her daughter, continued, "Mrs. Edwards even said she had some of your little drawings of her grandson. Perhaps I'll have you draw some of the children. You know the Reverend and I adopted a pair of twins. They're going to be a handful, I'm afraid. Raised Catholic so it will take some doing to convert them to Christianity," Mrs. Burgess said as if she saw nothing incongruous in what she had just conveyed.

"I'm sure you'll be able to bring them to the light, Mother. I wish you all the best and please let the Reverend and the others know I appreciated their acceptance and faith in me," Mary told this woman knowing, Mrs. Burgess was as good as she could be. "I hope to repay your kind deeds by doing more on my own. There will be missionary groups. I am sure I will be accepted since I speak several dialects of Apache and Numunuu."

"Numunuu, Mary? Who are they? I have never heard of them. Are they in Texas?" asked the older woman.

"It doesn't matter, Mother. I will send you my address when I get settled again. I am glad you were able to visit with me. Mrs. Brown has been more than generous in letting me stay here," Mary said as the woman who had been generous enough to adopt a Comanche captive rose to leave.

"Well, you are always welcomed home, crowded as it is. There could be room made for you," said Mrs. Burgess getting sentimental at the parting from this, her oldest daughter.

"I will keep that in mind. It is always good to have someplace to call home, but I am getting too old to remain a burden for you and the Reverend. I can make my way in the world now." And she did something she had never done before, she bent to kiss the soft cheek of her adoptive mother, who turned away embarrassedly with tears in her eyes.

CHAPTER FIFTEEN

The Major and Ben entered the ranch house after their three days away, surprising Emily and Jessie sitting in the living area knitting. The husbands went to their respective wives and kissed them in welcome. Morgan looked around the room and asked, "Mourning Dove upstairs?"

The room became silent and Emily volunteered, "She left with Nathan. He had taken all the photographs Jessie needed and was headed to Chicago to record the new buildings going up to replace the ones lost in the fire a few years ago. Some architectural firm is putting them in a brochure to be mailed internationally."

Morgan seemed stunned. "She simply left with him? Going to work beside him or something, then?"

"No, she didn't go with him in that way, Morgan. She thought there was nothing here for her. She wanted to learn to make her own way in this world. Nathan merely escorted her back to her home, back to where the Reverend and Mrs. Burgess live at the moment," Jessie interjected, wanting Morgan to know Mary hadn't gone with Nathan as a lover since she knew a little more about the two of them than the others.

Morgan nodded. "I'll check in with the chief and then probably head to Austin. I won't be here for meals, Mother, and I'm not sure when I'll return. When my work is done, I guess. Give William a kiss for me. I don't want to wake him since he's looking like such an angel."

212

Jessie nodded, knowing Morgan was on his way to bring Mary back using any method he could, even reverting back to his ancestors' methods of capturing women they wanted. Jessie hoped it wouldn't result in that.

Ben picked up his son, waking him up and receiving a rueful expression from his wife. The Major smiled and put out his arms, having missed holding his grandson and knowing Ben could hold him later when they all went to bed. Ben handed over his son to the waiting arms and the Major sat down next to his wife and shared his hard-won treasure with her. Ben sat next to Jessie, squeezing her into the corner of the wing backed chair, making Jessie drop her knitting in a knotted mess.

Later, after a meal thrown together of left over's and a couple of opened tin cans, the two couples went to bed, William soon fast asleep after a late feeding.

Ben confessed, "I missed you so much, Jessie. I don't sleep well when we're not together, no matter where that is.".

"Me, either. Do you think we'll get over that?" she asked him as she climbed into the bed wearing a thin muslin night gown tied at the neck with a ribbon.

"I hope not. I don't want you to take me for granted you know," teased Ben, pulling her closer, the most she allowed him to do since those weeks before the baby was born.

"I should take you for granted though, possibly every night. I'm the one not living up to my responsibilities. I'm simply afraid to resume our, well, letting you get so close again so soon. It only took one time together for you and me to make a baby and although I love him so very much, I don't want another child within a year of getting William."

Ben pulled her closer still and said quietly in his raspy voice, "I feel the same way. I mean, how can we give William the attention he needs right now if you were to become pregnant so soon. I worried about it, too. I even bought protection. You know, Goodyear rubbers to keep you from getting that way again right now."

"I've been unfair to you, Ben. Lately, I've looked at my life closer and find it isn't so different than what I always thought I wanted. Nathan reminded me how my parents worked together, but I think my mother gave up her life to live my father's. I don't remember them ever fighting or being discontent so I always thought they were happy. Now I think my mother would have been just as happy being a homemaker and mother to a brood of children."

"Is that what you want?" Ben had never heard Jessie question her plan before and he held back hope as to where this was going.

"I think there is room for both things in my life. A happy family, a loving husband, and my studies so that I never feel as if I've wasted my education. The ground work my father instilled in me."

"How do you see our lives going? More children mean we need to remain together." He tried not to let his voice show how close to perfect she was getting with her thoughts. She was sounding as if they had a shot at making their marriage work. Allow their love to flourish.

She stared into his eyes. "I don't want to be away from you. Our son will grow older and eventually leave to make his own way. You and I will need one another to have the strength to allow him that freedom. We need one another in different ways and I find I have such a love for you it takes my breath away."

He clutched her to his body. Ben's heart felt like it was bursting. These were the words he hoped to hear at some point in their relationship. Their passion freed and their wounds mended.

He couldn't keep his happiness from showing. "I want to be with you, always. I would keep our family together if you find you need to go somewhere dangerous. My parents would take care of them, but I will remain with you. I'll never allow you to go into danger without me."

"I understand. Having William makes me re-think the plans I made. There are enough endangered cultures for me to categorize without putting anyone in danger. We only have one life and I think my parents would agree with my plans to remain with you. I love you, Ben. I don't know why I've tried to hide it from you."

"Probably because you knew I'd try to keep you from doing foolish things. But if I couldn't, then I'd be by your side. And that's because I always knew I loved you. I came to ask you to marry me with my grandmother's rings in my pocket back in D. C. My doubts were never about whether or not we belonged together, but whether or not I could convince you we did."

"Oh, Ben, I'm sorry I didn't realize how much I loved you and being a mother before now. The other day, I was so worried for William and you I was sick with it. If you feel half of what I did, then I'm sorry for putting you through that."

"Now you know what my life is like. Thinking that you would tell me one day that you were ready to leave me. Forbid me from following. Forbid me from loving you."

Jessie gazed at her husband, "You never said anything. I guess I wasn't thinking about your needs in all this. I think my feeding William kind of tones down my wants and needs. I remember I was all over you most of the time in Florida."

"I live vicariously through those memories, hoping at some point you'll want to resume our normal activities. I'm ready whenever you are. I've just been glad to be allowed back into your bed. I sure as hell wasn't going to push my luck and urge you for more." Kissing her mouth and not being rejected, he asked to be sure, "Are you ready for more? It won't hurt you or anything?"

Jessie laughed and assured Ben, "No, it won't hurt me. In fact, if you do it right it's supposed to feel pretty good."

Ben rolled on top and buried his face in her neck kissing and sucking his way to her jaw and then lips as he showered her with all the passion he had been holding back, afraid to have her turn him away from her room, from her bed. Jessie seemed more than ready to pick up where they had left off, allowing Ben full access to her once forbidden body.

When Ben joined with Jessie, after putting on the protection, it was she who felt like they were coming home, becoming one as they were always meant to be. "I have missed this so much, Ben. I don't know why I thought I could ever leave you. Everyone was right. We belong together, as a family." She kissed his mouth as he began the long slow movements that had them both panting with passion as they reached the peak together.

CHAPTER SIXTEEN

Mrs. Brown came into Mary's room without knocking. "You have a visitor. I would appreciate you telling them to come to the rear door. It is quiet unsettling to find them on the front porch even if they are your relatives."

"I'm sorry you were disturbed, Mrs. Brown. I'll let them know the rules," Mary apologized, trying not to antagonize the woman who allowed her to have at least a semblance of independence.

Following the landlady out of the room, Mary went to the rear door, almost closing it immediately when she saw Morgan, hat in hand, standing outside waiting to speak with her. She had to be polite and talk with him or Mrs. Brown would think it suspicious.

"Morgan, you needn't have searched for me. I was planning on writing a letter to your mother as soon as I got settled," she said, smiling and longing to run anywhere out of his reach.

"I came for myself. I wanted, no, I needed to know you were all right. That you had enough money to take care of yourself, if there was anything you thought I should know about," he said evenly, letting her know he cared.

Mary's cheeks flushed and she stumbled with the answer, "I, I'm fine. Nothing you need to know about."

Morgan firmed his lips and then he asked outright, "Mourning Dove, are you with child? I deserve to know the truth."

"I am not with child and the truth is, I am probably barren. I was misused enough times I should have conceived when I was first taken and I didn't. I understand these things happen sometimes, nothing can be done about it," she said, keeping her head high, not letting him know how much this information hurt to tell him.

His eyes softened. "There's always adoption, Mourning Dove, I would love any child with you as my own. Marry me and come live with me in my tipi."

Mary's eye misted over and she asked, "Could you really live, knowing you would never have your own child?"

"I love William and he is so foreign to me I'm sometimes afraid to lift him even though I was there at his birth." He laughed at his own ill ease with his nephew.

"Why are you asking me this, knowing I'm not with child, knowing what you do about me?" she asked, gazing into his eyes searching for the truth.

"I have discovered my mother's side may be stronger than my father's. I want you with me, as my wife whether we live in a tipi, a fine Washington hotel or a ranch on my parent's land. You will have to be nomadic because I don't want to leave you behind, you and our children will travel with me, like a band of gypsies. Much like Ben and Jessie plan on doing, coming back to the ranch whenever there is a break in their work." He almost mashed the hat brim in his worry she would deny them this life.

"Are you in love with me?" she asked bravely.

"Of course, I am. I love you, Mourning Dove, and I want to marry you. I want to live with you forever. Is that plain enough for you?" he said, any chance the brim would survive gone as he clutched it waiting for her answer.

"Then I accept your proposal. I love you terribly and I was so miserable thinking I would never see you again. I felt like dying." She allowed her future husband to pick her up off the ground in a bear hug as he kissed the tears from her cheeks.

"That is so good to hear because I already told your parents when I got this address from them. The good Reverend Burgess was more than a little suspicious of my motives until I explained you were unsure of your feelings and came home to work them out. He seemed to think every young woman needs a man and finds me more than acceptable. Your mother helped him make up his mind. She seems to think my mother walks on water." He put Mary down but kept hold of her hands.

"I can pack right now and tell Mrs. Brown she'll have to get someone else to cook breakfast. I'll stay with my parents tonight," Mary said emphatically.

"No, we're going back to their house to be married by your father and then we will be on a train tonight heading back to Houston and then on to the ranch. I wasn't going to take no for an answer, I'm afraid. We became soul mates that night in my tipi. That's actually when I married you the first time. I've felt we've been a couple since then," he told her then urged her up the stairs to pack.

Mr. Toshawi Morgan and Mrs. Mourning Dove

Mary Morgan sat side by side in the train car, smiling every time their gazes met. Mourning Dove asked, "Do you know when you found out you loved me?"

"I can, it was a warm night in my tipi," he said, his lips lifting into a wide smile as he watched his bride of just a few hours blush.

"Are you going to keep harping on the one time I lost my inhibitions?" she scolded.

"Those memories were the only things that kept me sane while I saw you every day making moon-eyes at Nathan Fontaine. That man is lucky he still has all his parts," he threatened teasingly.

"I wasn't making moon-eyes. Honestly, that was merely your possessiveness making you see things. I never looked at him that way and he is half in love with Jessie. She, of course, only thinks of him as a friend," Mourning Dove said, thinking she was relaying news to Morgan.

"Personal relationships are complicated, but I'm glad I came to my senses in time to save us. If I had waited longer, we might have missed each other, you might have fallen in love with another man," he said, picking up her hand and kissing the back of it.

"Morgan, really. People might see," Mourning Dove said shyly, trying to pull her hand from his and then settled for bringing their hands down to rest between them.

"I'm having trouble waiting till we get home. I know I promised, but having you so close, so warm, so loving I'm getting into a rather difficult condition," he confessed, smiling at her high color.

She looked at her husband and then shook her head saying seriously, "This was your plan, now you will have to live with it. I'm waiting till we are safe and sound in our own tipi. Then you and I will wear the fur off those buffalo hides."

"What else could I expect of my Apache wife? I'm going to be sorry I told you we were waiting, but I think you plan on making it worth it for me." He smiled at her expression of disbelief that he would say such a thing out loud.

Emily came out drying her hands when she heard the unexpected buggy come down the drive to the kitchen door. "Mary, it's so good to see you again. Are you back for another visit?" She asked the couple, both wearing wide smiles.

"She's more than visiting, Mother, meet your new daughter-in-law, Mourning Dove Morgan. We were married by her father before we left town and then stopped by the camp where the medicine man blessed our union, too, so there isn't any chance of her leaving me." Morgan placed his hands on his wife's hips and lifted her down so Emily could hug her.

Jessie came out after hearing the commotion and greeted the married couple with squeals of joy, telling Mourning Dove she was so glad that Morgan found her and admitted his feelings. "I think we're finally getting a satisfactory balance now. There are three of us women and we can make the men behave," Jessie said, laughing at Morgan's expression of offended male pride.

Emily tried to make the dinner more festive than usual, but neither Morgan nor Mourning Dove drank more than a sip or two of the wine. Morgan peered over at his wife and received a shy peek in return. He knew she was thinking about being alone with him again.

"We'll see you in the morning, everyone. We plan on sleeping in the tipi until the cold weather drives us indoors. Thank you for the fine dinner, Mother," Morgan said, pulling out the chair for his wife so she could follow him.

Once in the tipi, Mourning Dove stood watching Morgan move their cases around and find another blanket. Emily had placed some flowers from the garden in a vase and left some food and beverages for them. "That was nice of your mother, to do this for us," she said as she knelt and smelled the flowers.

"She likes you, but of course she would, you are perfect," he said, taking off his coat and vest, hanging them from one of the poles. He followed those with his shirt and tie, unwinding the long black strip of material from around his tan neck. "Are you feeling afraid of me? You're not saying much and you keep searching around for an escape. If you're too tired we can simply go to sleep."

"No, I mean, I'm not afraid exactly, but I'm worried it won't be the same between us. Now that we're married it won't feel the same," she said, not meeting Morgan's gaze.

Still wearing his trousers, he crawled over to his wife and pulled her onto his lap which she did willingly. "I love you and that isn't an easy thing for me to say. You know that. I can wait until you're comfortable for us to make love again, but you seemed to enjoy it the last time. What do you think has changed?" he asked kissing her neck and jaw and cheek between words.

"You let me be in charge the first time and I liked that. I could stop if it got to be too much, but it was nice, being with you." Morgan waited to hear the rest and she began again, "The next time it was more as the Comanche do it, but with you it didn't scare me at all. I'm just afraid what the real you, wants.... I mean are you Comanche or White when we lay together?"

"I'm your husband, Mourning Dove, I'm never going to hurt you. As far as making love, this next time I think it should be as a Whiteman. Does that sound interesting?" he said as she raised her head allowing him access to her throat as he slowly unbuttoned the front of her dress and slipped his hand in to massage her eager breast, the nipple turning pebble hard at his touch.

"You need to let me know what you like and compliment me when I please you. I have it on the best of authority, this is how the Whiteman does it," he said as he nipped and sucked at her skin.

"I like everything you're making me feel, lazy and cherished and loved. I couldn't ask for more," she whispered to him.

Mourning Dove turned more toward him and kissed his mouth, holding his head to her with her arms as he laid them down on the brightly striped blanket. He untied the camisole allowing more access for his mouth and tongue to explore her breasts which caused her to arch up, offering him whatever he wanted. He unbuttoned the waist of her skirts and pulled everything up over her head, leaving her wearing stockings, which he rolled down, stroking her long bare legs as he returned to suckle at her breast. Morgan kissed his way down her body and when his lips met the apex of her thighs his wife tensed.

"Let me love you. I have it on the best of authority this is how the Whiteman does it." He felt her relax as his tongue slid into her warmth, one finger sliding in and out of her already slick channel.

"I like this, too. I would never have believed I would have enjoyed such a thing, but this is nice, this is very, very nice," she moaned. It wasn't long before Mourning Dove stiffened with an orgasm, making Morgan smile in satisfaction.

Pushing down his trousers, he kicked them off as he climbed back to be level with his wife, who was still in a blissful haze accepting his kisses. She stroked her hands over his muscled arms and shoulders, finding the familiar about this man she loved.

"I have it on the best of authority this is how the Whiteman does it. Their women enjoy multiple orgasms when they make love," he said as he again suckled at each breast, one then the other, his palm stroking the mound he had just pleasured.

"I like the Whiteman's way so far. Is there more I should be doing?" she asked, letting her hands travel over his chest as she licked his nipples and felt their immediate response.

"I'm enjoying everything, too. I don't think I can keep holding back much longer. It seems it all boils down to me being inside of you, like a hand in a glove." He entered her, setting a leisurely pace for them that soon sped up until they both shuddered into a mutual climax bringing them to a euphoric conclusion as Morgan collapsed on to his wife, keeping his weight off her as much as he was able.

When they were able to catch their breath, Morgan hugged his wife to him and asked teasingly, "Well, now, which way do you want me to make love to you?"

Mourning Dove smiled and said as seriously as she could, "I might need to compare them, you know side by side."

Laughing and rolling her on top of him, Morgan said, "We may have to wait a moment or two before we see how well you remember your part."

"I'll always remember my part. I'm the one who is so lucky to have found you, to be brought back to my heritage, to a man who understands me so well," she said as she kissed him, sucking his lip into her mouth, feeling as he became aroused beneath her.

"I'm the lucky one, you came and saved me from turning into a one-sided man. I now feel I have a life, a future, and I'm not simply trying to save a dying people," he explained what he was feeling, letting her know how much he felt she was giving him beside her body to love.

He asked, lifting his hips letting her know he was ready to make love in any manner she wanted. "Are you ready to compare now?"

EPILOGUE

The cold air tried to find its way through to Jessie's skin. "It's remarkable these huge mammals never come out of the water other than the times they are showing off for us," Jessie said as she watched the large pod of whales play with each other in the cold Alaskan sea. "It's a shame Mourning Dove was just delivered of her daughter. She and Morgan would have enjoyed this trip. Maybe next time and the children will keep each other company."

Ben answered, "Hmmm, if you say so. William and I think it's too early to do anything besides have breakfast which I enjoy feeding to him now that he's weaned." He tweaked his son's little red nose as his mother held him so that he could see the huge mammoths frolic alongside the cruise ship they were travelling on.

The three of them were wrapped in a large buffalo robe Morgan had given them for this trip to study the Inuit in Alaska for the summer. Their first true anthropological assignment away from home. Jessie knew it had been her in-depth study of the Numunuu that had the museum agree so heartily about her travelling to Alaska after having a family. They may not understand her life, but they couldn't fault it as having held her back, either. Another thing, she had Morgan to thank for although she took credit for pushing him towards Mary. For making him realize there could be more to his life, if he thought Jessie could be a wife, mother and anthropologist.

As William got older, Jessie and Ben decided the trip to Alaska was safe enough for the family and there was little illness up here. In fact, the family from Texas was more of a danger to the aboriginal Inuit than the other way around. Jessie was going to keep William away from the Inuit for a couple of weeks to be sure he wasn't carrying any childhood diseases before introducing him to the local children.

Ben leaned down asking, "Do you think we can sneak back into our cabin and maybe come up with something to entertain us more than the leaping whales?" He pulled her into his arousal.

"Honestly Ben, do you ever think about anything else?" she said, laughing and trying to straighten herself away from her amorous husband while peering around at the other ship's travelers.

"I used to, I think, but now I'm not sure. I know that's all I think about lately so maybe you should run a study. You know put a grid on me and study me and take notes. I'll help you with the drawings."

"I'll send you to the brig, if you don't stop nudging me," she threatened.

With a straight face he said, "I'm not nudging you." Under cover of the buffalo robe she slapped his hand away as it went to fondle her breast, a breast that was now free for his pleasure since William was eating solid foods.

"Stop misbehaving, you fool," she said, laughing.

"Yes, but I'm your fool." he said into her ear, loving the fact he could still make her blush.

The people on the bridge were beginning to walk away, now the whales had gone in a different direction. Jessie turned to her husband. "Well, are you going to put up or shut up?" She watched his eyes light with desire as he realized he may get her back into the cabin yet.

"I'll do either one, which ever gets me my heart's desire," he told her truthfully.

"And that would be…?" she asked not sure where he was going with this.

"A sister or brother for William? I hear only children can become overly demanding and self-centered and bossy," he further teased his wife.

"Bossy? They get bossy?" she said, falling on the bed once they reached their cabin.

"I didn't say it was a bad thing," he told her, setting William where he couldn't get hurt and going to lay down on the bed next to her.

"So, you think we should start on a sibling for William, do you? Well, one in Texas and one in Alaska Territory, that should cover the ones conceived in North America. Are the others going to be by country or continents and don't forget the oceans?" She began to count those, but soon ran out of fingers.

"All right you win, we will be a little selective. But I think one from the Alaskan Territory is a good place to start." He was kissing her neck, fondling her, seeking more intimate areas.

"Then we will have to wait until we find us an igloo."

"A what? Is that like a tipi?"

"Close, but it's made of ice and snow and I understand they sleep in them naked."

"I like the naked part, but they are really made out of ice and snow?" He hoped body parts weren't shriveling as he thought about the home he was going to have to live in for the next four months.

"Relax, we'll be in a cabin, but I want you to be on your best behavior while we're up here. I've heard they also share their women to visitors to help warm their beds." She watched him closely as he refused any emotions to cross his face.

"I don't have to reciprocate, do I?" he asked weakly, unconsciously pulling her to him.

"No, we won't be expected to participate at all. I'm just forewarning you now in case what I've heard is true." She kissed his mouth to make him shut it.

"I think I like our way best. I just found out I'm a very possessive fellow." He rolled on top of her as their son slept peacefully in his bunk.

"I love you."

"I love you so much more." Ben said. "And to think I almost let Meijer's take you into the desert on that field trip."

"Our lives would have been much less satisfactory."

"H-m-m-m-m. Satisfaction."

A word about the author...

A voracious reader her whole life, author Susan Payne loved the written word. When reading more than fifty books per month wasn't enough, she decided to allow her mind to take flight and write all the many stories that kept intruding into her life. She blended her love of history and her love of words to create over eighty stories. All historical and centering on a couple finding love and a happy ever after together.

You may contact Susan at:
http://www.authorsusanpayne.com or
authorspayne@gmail.com

Thank you for purchasing
this publication of The Wild Rose Press, Inc.

For questions or more information
contact us at
info@thewildrosepress.com.

The Wild Rose Press, Inc.
www.thewildrosepress.com